The Ballet Blues

Lily couldn't think of anywhere in the world she wanted to go less than Capezio, unless maybe it was to the dentist or to dancing school itself, and she knew very well that if she went to Capezio, she'd probably end up going to dancing school. Anything but that. Let Saundra go to dancing school. Saundra *belonged* at dancing school. Lily didn't. She hardly belonged anywhere that Saundra was. She didn't even belong in the same bedroom with her.

THE SISTERS IMPOSSIBLE

James David Landis

BULLSEYE BOOKS · ALFRED A. KNOPF

NEW YORK

for Sara Cass Landis

A BULLSEYE BOOK PUBLISHED BY ALFRED A. KNOPF, INC.
Copyright © 1979 by James David Landis
Cover art copyright © 1991 by Bill Donahey

Library of Congress Catalog Card Number: 78-32148
ISBN: 0-679-80219-3
RL: 4.8
First Bullseye Books edition: January 1991

Manufactured in the United States of America
10 9 8 7 6 5 4 3 2 1

Contents

·1·
Put on Your Dancing Shoes

"Put on your dancing shoes, Lily," said Lily's father, who was wearing his brand-new green jogging shoes, made by Adidas, and his brand-new jogging suit, made of shiny red nylon, bright in the sunlight coming into their living room.

"I don't have any dancing shoes, Dad," Lily said. And I don't want any, either, she thought but did not say.

"It's only an expression," her father said.

"What does it mean?" Lily asked.

"It means . . . it means *put on your dancing shoes.* It means *have a good time.*"

"I am having a good time. Besides, you can't go dancing in a jogging suit."

"And you, young lady, can't go dancing in a bathrobe."

"But I don't want to go dancing," said Lily, tightening the sash of her bathrobe.

"And I don't want to go jogging. At least, I don't think I want to go jogging. But how should I know? I've never been jogging in my life. Nothing ventured, nothing gained. Not that I have to gain anything." He patted his round stomach, which made the red nylon curve like a balloon.

Lily pictured a balloon rolling around the Central Park reservoir, passing the other joggers, who stopped in their tracks at seeing a balloon that could run faster than they could. She giggled.

"What's so funny?" asked her father. "I'm not *that* fat. And when I'm done jogging—"

"You'll take me for a walk?" Lily asked.

"I will?"

"Will you? Please. To a museum?"

"I'll be too skinny to take you for a walk."

"Too skinny?"

"Well . . ." Her father started to rotate his arms. He looked like a windmill. "I'll—be—too—tired," he said, puffing.

"What are you doing with your arms?" Lily asked.

"I'm—warming—up," he said.

"Are you going to run on your arms?"

"Don't—be—funny . . ."

"My dad," said Lily, "the running windmill."

"Very funny," said her father sarcastically. He stopped rotating his arms and began to lift his legs up and down, one after the other.

"What are you doing now?" Lily asked.

"I'm—still—warming—up. I'm—running—in—place."

"But you're not going anywhere."

"Phew," said her father. He was beginning to huff and puff. Also, his face was turning as red as his jogging suit.

"You better stop, Dad."

"Why?" he asked, still bouncing up and down. Now he looked like a balloon on a windy day. "Phew."

"I'm afraid you'll pop," Lily said.

"Don't call me Pop," he said. "Call me Dad."

"Very funny," said Lily sarcastically.

"You dish it out, you've got to take it," he said. He was breathing hard now. His stomach rose and fell inside the red jogging suit. He opened his arms to give her a hug. "Wish me luck, kiddo," he said.

Lily took one step backward. "You're sweaty," she said.

"A good sign," he said. "I'm already beginning to lose weight." He touched her nose with his finger. His finger was dry, so Lily pushed her nose against it and wiggled her face. "Wish me luck," he said again.

"Good luck," she said.

"Put on your dancing shoes, Lily," her father said.

He started to run through the living room toward

the door of their apartment. Lily wondered if he was going to take the elevator down the ten flights or was planning to run down the back stairs. She hoped he would take the elevator. If he ran down the stairs, he might fall. And that would be the end of his jogging. She pictured him rolling down the ten flights of stairs. At that very moment, he tripped on the edge of the rug and almost fell down right on the living-room floor. He was as clumsy as she was. That was one of the reasons she loved him so much.

"Take the elevator, Dad," she said.

"Good idea," he said. He didn't turn to look at her. He was probably too embarrassed at nearly having fallen on the floor in his brand-new jogging suit. "I hope there aren't people on it," he said.

"So what if there are?"

"I look silly," her father said. Now he turned to look at her. He ran his hands up and down his jogging suit. "Look at me," he said. Then he laughed. "I look silly. I look like Santa Claus."

"No you don't," she said.

"I don't?"

"You look like a red balloon."

"Oh, thanks, kiddo. What a compliment. But just you wait."

"For what?"

"When I come home," he said, "I'm going to look like Nureyev."

"Who's that?" Lily asked, even though she thought

she knew, because her sister had mentioned that name so often.

"The dancer!" her father said. "The greatest!"

"Oh," said Lily. She *had* remembered.

"Just you wait," he said. "I'll be home soon. You'll see. Harold Nureyev." He tried to stand on his tiptoes and twirl around. He nearly fell down again. "Put on your—"

"—dancing shoes," said Lily.

"No," said her father. "Put on your clothes. Put on your walking shoes. When I come home, we *are* going out for a walk."

"Oh, goody," said Lily.

"But not to a museum. I'm taking you to Capezio. I'm going to buy you a present."

"What?" asked Lily.

"Dancing shoes," her father said. "You're going to take dancing lessons."

Before Lily could protest, he was out the door. The last thing she saw was the heel of one of his green shoes. Red and green—her father certainly was a colorful character. She hoped he wouldn't fall down on the jogging track. She didn't want him to be embarrassed. She wanted him to hurry up and come home.

·2·
So What?

Lily didn't want to go to Capezio. She knew what Capezio was. It was a store for dancers. Dancers went there and bought leotards and tights and dancing shoes.

Lily knew all about Capezio. Her sister, Saundra, practically lived there—there and at her dancing school.

Saundra wanted to be a ballerina.

Skinny Saundra. Pretty Saundra. Graceful Saundra.

Her middle name was Rose. But it should have been Capezio. Saundra Capezio Leonard. Who left her tights and leotards all over the bathroom, and her Capezio bags all over the floor of the bedroom they shared.

Saundra might be skinny and beautiful and grace-ful. But she certainly accumulated a lot of junk. And Lily had to live with it. She was constantly tripping over it and sitting on it by mistake and sometimes even smelling it, when it was sweaty old leotards and tights that Saundra had stuffed into her Capezio bags and had forgotten.

Lily had reached the conclusion that a person might indeed be skinny and beautiful and graceful, but this still didn't mean that this person wasn't a slob.

Saundra was a slob. Maybe Lily was the only one who knew it. But she knew it.

Lily, on the other hand, was not a slob. She was very neat. She put her clothes away in her drawer. She lined up her sneakers in her closet. She made her bed every morning. She folded her towel after she dried her face. And she always brushed her hair, even if brushing it did no good.

So why was it that everyone thought Saundra was the neatest, cleanest, most graceful, most organized young lady in the whole world? Why was it that everyone thought she, Lily, was the messy one?

It wasn't fair.

Maybe it was her hair. Lily's hair was thick and curly, a kind of reddish blond that flew all over the place no matter how much she brushed it and no matter how tightly she pulled it back from her forehead and up from her ears before securing it with rubber bands. Saundra's hair was straight and smooth and dark, and all Saundra had to do was grab her hair in one hand and slip a ribbon around it with the other, and it sat on the top of her head in a neat bun without a single strand sticking out on the sides or back.

Maybe it was her face. Lily's face was round and soft and pink; it went from expression to expression, each one dreamy and smiley, like a ball bouncing down a hill and unable to stop. Saundra's face was long and thin and pale and seemed to have only one expression: haughty. Once, in the middle of the night, Lily got out of her bed and tiptoed to Saundra's bed and put her face close to her sister's face and looked very closely to see how Saundra looked when she was asleep. Saundra's face still had only one expression: haughty. Lily couldn't bear it any longer. She stood there bent over her sister, looking at her face in the dim light from the moon and the streetlamp and began to make funny faces right in Saundra's face. Saundra didn't change her expression. Lily stuck out her tongue at Saundra, but Saundra didn't change her expression. Finally, Lily let her tongue touch her sister's nose and at the same time took a deep breath and blew as hard as she could. Saundra woke with a start that made Lily jump back. "What are you doing?" Saundra asked. "Nothing," said Lily. "Did you put something on my face?" asked Saundra. "No," said Lily. "Why are you standing so close to me?" asked Saundra. "I'm looking at you," said Lily. "Do I look nice?" asked Saundra. Lily didn't answer.

"Do I look nice?" Saundra asked again. Again Lily said nothing. "I've often wondered what I look like when I'm asleep. Tell me how I look," Saundra demanded. "The same as always," Lily said, and went back to her own bed.

Or maybe it was her body. Her body and the way she dressed. Saundra was tall and skinny, Lily was shorter and, well, just a bit chubby. Of course, it was perfectly natural that Lily at nine years old was shorter than Saundra at fourteen. "You're my huggable bug," her father said about Lily, and it was true that people liked to hug Lily more than they did Saundra. But the hugs weren't worth it. Lily didn't want people to hug her. She wanted people to say she was beautiful. She didn't want her mother to say she was "unusual-looking." She wanted her mother to call her what she called Saundra: "stunning."

Maybe it really was the way she dressed. Lily wore sweatshirts all the time, winter and summer, with baggy jeans or baggy overalls, and except in the deepest snow she wore sneakers. Saundra wore leotards almost constantly. And when she wore jeans they weren't baggy but very tight. They came from the French Jean Store, and each pair had a foreign name on the back pocket or up near the belt loops. "Forty dollars for a pair of jeans!" their father would say whenever Saundra came home with a new pair. Then her mother would say to their father as Saundra modeled her new jeans, "Do you think they look beautiful on her?" And their father would reply, "Sure. She looks like a million bucks. Unfortunately, I don't have a million bucks." But his smile at seeing Saundra in her jeans would show everyone that he knew Saundra was beautiful. And dressing her so that she looked beautiful was, as he sometimes said, "worth every penny—and that's a whole lot of pennies for a pair of pants."

It wasn't fair, Lily thought. None of it was fair.

So what if she and her sister looked so different that no one could believe that they were sisters, and people said to Saundra, when they met Lily, "She's your *sister!*"? So what if Saundra was skinny and pretty and graceful, and Lily was round and huggable and clumsy?

So everything. Oh. So everything.

·3·
Ugly Feet

When her father came home from his jog, Lily was putting on her "walking shoes"—her beloved sneakers—and at the same time rehearsing what she would say to him so that he would take her out for a walk, but not to Capezio. She couldn't think of anywhere in the world she wanted to go less than to Capezio, unless maybe it was to the dentist or to dancing school itself, and she knew very well that if she went to Capezio, she'd probably end up going to dancing school. Anything but that. Anything. Let Saundra go to dancing school. Saundra *belonged* at dancing school. Lily didn't. She hardly belonged anywhere that Saundra was. She didn't even belong in the same bedroom with her.

"Hi, Dad," Lily said when she saw her father going past her door. "How was it?"

He peered in at her. His face was nearly as red as his new jogging suit. It was also just as shiny, because he was sweating. He leaned against the doorway and looked as if he'd like to slide right down it into a heap on the floor.

"How was it, Dad?" she asked again.

"Phew," he said.

"How do you feel?"

"Phew," he said again.

"Did you make it around the reservoir?"

"Don't ask," he said.

"I guess you didn't," Lily said.

"I didn't," he answered.

"Don't worry."

"Who said I'm worried?"

"You look worried," Lily said, because his face was sad.

"I'm not worried. I'm exhausted. And my feet hurt." He lifted one of his feet and put his hand around the green sneaker so that his fingers pressed his little toe. "I think I worked up a blister," he said.

"That's a good sign," Lily said.

"Is it?" He put his foot down and looked right into her eyes. "How can it be a good sign? It just means I'm soft. A blister can't be a good sign of anything."

"But it means you'll get a callus there. Saundra says she sometimes gets blisters on her feet. And then, in a few days, she says there's a callus in the very same place, and it's as hard as a stone."

"And ugly," her father said.

"What?" Lily said. She had never heard him use that word about anything. It sounded very strange coming from his mouth. It was almost as if he had said a swear word.

"Dancers have ugly feet," he said, using the word again as if it were the most natural thing in the world to say it.

Lily still couldn't believe her ears. "Do you think Saundra has ugly feet?" she asked.

"All dancers have ugly feet," he said. "It's part of the price they pay."

"For what?"

"For being beautiful," her father said. Then he groaned softly and pushed his body away from its resting place against the doorway and stood there on his own two feet. "Phew," he said, "am I worn out."

Lily wanted to ask him again if he really thought Saundra had ugly feet, and if she did, what did that really have to do with being beautiful? But instead she bent down to tie her sneaker and said, "Are we still going out for a walk?"

"No," he said.

Lily felt a strange sense of disappointment mingled with an equally strange sense of relief. She had been looking forward to the walk with her father, but she had been dreading the place they were going to walk to: Capezio. She realized that her disappointment was greater than her relief. She felt like crying. Instead she began to untie her sneaker.

"But don't take off your shoes," her father said.

"Why not?" She said it angrily.

"Because you'll still need something on your feet in the taxi." He smiled at her. "I may not be able to walk there," he said, "but that doesn't mean we aren't going."

He started to go down the hall. Lily noticed he was limping. She got up and started to walk after him—and she realized that she was limping too, because she still had on only one sneaker.

"Wait a minute," she said.

He turned around and looked at her impatiently. "I really need a shower," he said. "I'm hot. I'm exhausted. And I probably smell. Can it wait until I'm done?"

Lily shook her head. "I know what Capezio is," she said.

"I know you know," he said, starting to turn back toward the bathroom at the end of the hall. "I know you know," he said again.

"Well, I don't want to go there," she said.

Again he turned back toward her. "I know you don't. So far, Lily, you haven't told me anything I don't already know. And if I don't get into a shower soon, I'm going to be so stiff you're going to have to roll me to Capezio."

"But I don't want to go to Capezio!"

"I know, I know," he said. "But tell me something. Where would you rather go: to Capezio or to dancing school?"

"To Capezio," Lily said without a moment's hesitation.

"Well, then," her father said, "you're in luck. Because that's where we're going."

"Then I don't have to go to dancing school?" Lily asked.

"Now did I say that?" her father said, and this time he turned around and walked away and went right into the bathroom and closed the door.

Lily stood completely still, unable to believe that he had disappeared so fast. She looked at the bathroom door and said to herself, He *tricked* me, and at that very moment the door opened a crack. Steam poured out, but she could still see her father's red face.

"I'm sorry I tricked you," he said. "It wasn't very nice." Then the door closed as quickly as it had opened.

It was as if he could read her mind. Waiting for him, she listened to the water from his shower and wondered why she had never noticed that Saundra had ugly feet.

·4·
You Have to Dance to Be a Dancer

Capezio was a madhouse. Lily's father pulled open the door for her—he was always the gentleman—and she walked in, turning sideways to avoid a girl and her mother who were walking out. But before her father could get in, a whole group of girls took advantage of the open door and walked out in a line—and all the while Lily's father was holding open the door. Out they went, clutching their Capezio bags and talking, and never saying thank you to the man who was holding the door.

Lily watched her father stand there helplessly as the girls filed out. She wanted to go up to them and tell them to say thank you, tell them that the man holding the door for them was not a doorman but a lawyer.

"May I help you?" someone asked her.

Lily turned, and saw right in front of her a belt, a belt that was holding up a skirt. The belt was just level with her eyes. Lily looked down and saw a pair of boots. Lily looked up—up past a leotard that was tucked into the skirt—and saw, way above her, one of the tallest people she had ever seen.

"You can help *him*," she said, pointing to her father.

"I beg your pardon," the tall woman said.

"Him," Lily said, pointing to her father, who was now trying to edge through the door without bumping into the people still walking out.

"He seems to be stuck," the woman said. "Is he trying to come in or go out?"

"I wish he were trying to go out," Lily said.

"A relative of yours?" the woman asked.

"Oh, no," said Lily.

"No?"

"Just my father," Lily said.

"I see," said the woman.

Lily looked up at her face, which looked down at Lily with a puzzled expression. Lily gave the woman a smile, and the woman gave Lily a smile. Which wasn't easy. The woman's hair was pulled back so tightly that the smile must have hurt her face, for she suddenly stopped smiling and a look of pain came into her eyes.

"What's the matter?" Lily asked.

"Your father . . ." the woman said. "He really seems to be stuck. His foot. Why don't you give him a hand?"

"Will you wait on us?" Lily asked.

"Of course," said the woman. "What is it you'll be wanting?"

"My father wants to buy a pair of tights," Lily said.

"Tights?" the woman said. "Isn't he a bit—?"

"My father is a great dancer," Lily said.

"He is? But isn't he a bit—?"

"He had to gain some weight for his newest role," Lily explained.

"What's he playing? Humpty Dumpty?" She laughed.

"Very funny," said Lily, laughing herself. "Will you wait on us?" she asked again.

"Sure," said the woman. "I'll go check out our supply of jumbo tights." She walked away, shaking her head.

Lily went over to her father.

"Did you see what happened to my foot?" he asked.

"What?"

"It got caught in the door."

"Did it hurt?"

"A little bit," he said, lifting his foot and shaking it. "I think it got swollen from running."

"Did you squash your blister in the door?"

"My blister's on the other foot."

"*Yikes*," said Lily. "Both feet. I guess we'll be taking a taxi home, too."

"Two taxis," said her father.

"Two?" said Lily, thinking he was going to put her

in a taxi all by herself. Maybe he was going to his office. Or maybe to a foot doctor.

"One for each foot," her father said with a twinkle in his eye. Then he gave her cheek a little touch, to show he was teasing. "Now, let's get you some dancing shoes."

"Let's not," Lily said.

"I can see you need a push," he said.

She certainly didn't want him to push her around the store, so she took his hand and pulled *him* through the crowd of people, most of whom seemed to be skinny, haughty girls just like Saundra. Some of them were alone, and some were with their mothers. Lily's father was about the only man in the store. Even the few little boys were there with their mothers.

"Here we are," Lily said to the tall woman when they finally reached her.

"I'm sorry, sir," the woman said to Lily's father.

"For what?" he asked.

"I'm not sure we can fit you."

"Me?" he said.

"The tights for your role," the woman explained.

"*My* tights! Me? Tights? I'm sorry, but I'm afraid—"

"I'm afraid too," the tall woman interrupted him. She looked past him and gave Lily a little wink. She was trying very hard not to smile. "I'm afraid we may not be able to fit you."

"But you don't understand," Lily's father said,

scratching his head, because *he* didn't understand.

"Oh, I understand. You won't be able to dance your role unless you can find a pair of tights. Well, if Capezio doesn't have your tights, then no one does. And if no one has your tights, then you won't be able to dance your role."

"What role? What tights?"

"Jumbo tights, Dad," Lily said.

"Jumbo tights!" he said.

The tall woman couldn't contain herself any longer. She started to laugh. Through her laughter, she said, "Humpty Dumpty." That made her laugh even harder. It also made Lily laugh.

"Whoty whoty?" asked Lily's father. Then he started to laugh. He finally realized that they were teasing him.

"Humpty Dumpty," Lily said.

"That's what I thought you said," her father said. Then he looked up at the tall woman. "It's my most famous role," he told her.

"I can imagine," said the woman, looking him up and down.

"But I don't need jumbo tights any longer." He put both hands on his round belly.

"You could have fooled me," said the tall woman.

"I needed them this morning. But I don't need them now. And do you know why I don't need them now?" He didn't wait for them to answer. "I don't need them now because I went jogging this morning. *Before* I went jogging, I needed jumbo tights. But now that I've gone jogging, I need only extra-large tights. Do you have any extra-large tights?"

"Why, I think we do," said the woman.

"Good," said Lily's father. "I'll take one pair of extra-large tights. And we'll have one pair of dancing shoes for Lily."

"Dad, *please* . . ." Lily said. Why couldn't he just buy his tights and then take her home, even in a taxi—even in two taxis? Why did he have to remember the shoes?

"I'll find your tights," said the woman. She turned to go, then turned back again and looked directly at Lily, who looked up and met the woman's eyes, which were beautiful even if they did have too much makeup on them. "Lily," she said, "don't be afraid to buy shoes. I'll help you pick them out." The woman turned around again and started to make her way through the crowd of girls and boys and their mothers to find the tights for Lily's father.

"Are you afraid?" her father asked.

"I don't know," said Lily.

"What are you afraid of?"

"I'm not afraid. I just don't want dancing shoes."

"Why not?"

"I don't want to dance."

"Are you sure you don't?"

"One dancer in the family is enough," Lily said.

"Two would be nicer," her father said.

"Why?" asked Lily. "Why would two be nicer? One father in the family is enough. Two fathers in the family would *not* be nicer. So why do we need two dancers?"

Her father seemed perplexed. Then he said, "I know what you should be."

"What?" asked Lily, afraid he was going to say something about dancing.

"A lawyer," he said.

"Really?" Lily was pleased. "Why do you say that?"

"Because you're the only person who can argue a point better than I can," he said, reaching down and putting his fingers into her curly hair.

"Don't touch the merchandise," Lily said.

This expression was just one more joke the two of them shared. Actually, Lily loved the feel of his hand on her head. Almost as much as she loved arguing a point better than he could. Nine years old and already smart enough to be a lawyer. She only wished she could dance.

The tall woman returned with a pair of red tights. "Here you are," she said, handing them to Lily's father. "One pair of extra-large tights."

"Extra large," Lily said, laughing.

"What's so funny?" her father asked.

"Extra large," Lily repeated. "You're fat!" She laughed again.

"Not funny," said her father. His faced looked sad.

"I'm sorry," Lily apologized. She knew it was unkind to make fun of someone else, especially in public.

"I think she's angry with you," the tall woman said to Lily's father.

"No, she's not," he said to her.

"She's right, Dad," Lily said.

"You're angry with me? Why?"

Lily didn't answer.

The tall woman answered for her. "I don't think Lily wants to buy shoes."

"I know she doesn't," he said. "But that's a ridiculous attitude."

"No, it isn't," said the tall woman. "A lot of girls and boys are brought in here by their parents. They don't want to come. They're dragged in. Why? Because their parents want them to dance. The *children* don't want to dance. Their *parents* want them to dance. And if that's the case, they don't need dancing shoes."

"Some saleswoman you are!" said Lily's father.

"I'd rather see a happy child than sell a pair of shoes," the woman said.

"Just because Lily doesn't want the shoes doesn't mean they won't make her happy," he said.

"I don't understand," said the tall woman.

"Well," he said, rubbing his two hands together, the way he always did when he was about to make a speech. "I agree with you that sometimes parents want children to dance, and the children don't want to. But there are a lot of things children don't want to do. Or they *think* they don't want to do them. But once they start to do them, they love to do them. Someone has to start them. Someone has to give them a little push. And that someone is usually their parents. If parents didn't push their children into things, their children might not do anything."

"So you want to push Lily into dancing?" the woman asked.

"I don't *want* to push her. But if she needs a little push . . ."

"What do you say, Lily?" the tall woman asked her.

Lily knew it was hopeless to argue with her father. Besides, maybe he was right. Maybe she did need a little push. Maybe, once she started to dance, she would learn how and not feel so clumsy and would be good at it and would love it. Maybe she would even be better than Saundra.

She held her arms up in the air and said, "Give me a push, Dad."

"That's my girl," he said to her, resting his hand on her shoulders. And to the tall woman he said, "Show us the shoes!"

The woman smiled, took Lily's hand, and led her through the crowd to two chairs, where Lily sat with her father. The woman left them, to return in a few minutes with an armful of boxes. She opened the boxes one after the other and showed Lily jazz shoes made of leather and looking like sneakers; tap-dancing shoes, which had ribbons and were made of shiny patent leather; point shoes, of pink satin, just like Saundra's; and ballet slippers in white, pink, and black.

Deep down, Lily most wanted the point shoes, but she knew they were not for beginners. The tall woman said as much when she said that Lily was not strong enough for them yet.

Next Lily wanted jazz shoes, because they looked most like her beloved sneakers. But her father merely said, "Jazz shoes!" shook his head, and that was that.

After jazz shoes, Lily wanted tap-dancing shoes, because she liked the ribbon, and she liked the metal taps on the heel and toe of each shoe, and she could picture herself tap dancing through the halls at school in the fall. "Tap shoes!" her father said. This time he didn't even bother to shake his head. And that was that.

"What color ballet slippers would you like?" the tall woman asked her.

"Black," Lily said.

"Black!" her father said.

"Black," said Lily.

Her father raised his eyebrows, but he didn't say anything else.

That is how Lily got her dancing shoes.

"Good luck," said the tall woman as she handed Lily a black-and-white Capezio bag.

Inside the bag were her black ballet slippers, black tights, and a black leotard.

"Thank you," said Lily.

"I like you, Lily," said the tall woman. "I hope you'll be a good dancer. Even if you're not, I hope you'll enjoy dancing. But if you're not a good dancer, and you don't enjoy dancing, I hope you'll stop dancing and do something else."

"Why did you stop dancing?" Lily asked her.

"Me?" said the tall woman. "Oh, I don't dance. I never danced."

"But you look so much like a dancer," Lily said.

The tall woman smiled down at her. "Ah, yes," she said. "I know. I'm tall, and I stand up straight, and I wear my hair in a bun, and I walk with my head thrown back and my shoulders out and my stomach in and my hands held in loose curves like the neck of a goose. I do look like a dancer."

"But you're not?" asked Lily. "Really?"

"Really," said the woman. "I never danced in my life. But I look like a dancer. That's how I got this job at Capezio. If I were a dancer, I would be dancing, not working in a dance store. Real dancers dance. That's all they do. Dance. But not me. I don't dance. I just look like a dancer. Almost anyone can look like a dancer. But very few can actually dance. I hope you'll be one of them, if that's what you really want."

"I don't know if it is," Lily said.

"How could you?" said the woman. "You've never danced."

"That's true," said Lily. And she thought, maybe when she actually danced, maybe when she actually put on her tights and her leotard and her new black ballet slippers, she would really dance and be good and love it.

"Well, good luck," said the tall woman again. She bent down, as if she were a tree tipping over from the sky just where her branches joined her trunk, and gave Lily a kiss on the cheek. "Remember: You don't have to be a dancer to look like a dancer. But you do have to dance to be a dancer. Dance, Lily. Dance."

Lily's father held open the door for her. She held on to his hand and pulled him through right after her, so he wouldn't get stuck again holding the door for all the other girls and boys marching in and out of Capezio trying to be dancers, just like her.

Sides

"Lily's going to study dancing!"

They were sitting around the dinner table, eating shrimp salad and drinking iced tea and chilled white wine because of the heat of this early summer evening.

"That's right," said Lily's father.

"Lily's going to study dancing!" Saundra said again. This time she shook her head.

"She sure is," said their father.

"Where?"

"The American Ballet Center," he said.

"You've got to be kidding," Saundra said.

"Nope," said their father.

"Mom," said Saundra and looked pleadingly at their mother. For the first time Lily could remember, her sister slumped in her chair.

Their mother was supposed to be the decision-maker in the family. Like their father, she was a lawyer. But she was also a judge. So no one referred to her any longer as a lawyer. Now everyone thought of her as, and called her, a judge: Judge Leonard. Their father loved the fact that his wife was a judge, especially when people made a mistake and thought *he* was the judge. At such times, he pointed to his wife and said, "*This* is Judge Leonard," and smiled mischievously. People still weren't used to women judges, and Mr. Leonard enjoyed seeing their surprised confusion.

When serving in court, Judge Leonard was decisive, as Lily knew from hearing her father describe the cases over which her mother presided. She was known throughout the city as Judge Forget-Me-Not, because she never forgot anything, not a fact, not a face, and certainly not people who spoke too slowly or could not make up their minds.

"Your mother," their father had told them more than once, "is the hardest thing in court, aside from the benches." Then he would put his hands on his behind, to make them laugh.

But at home—at home, she was different. At home, she was *supposed* to be the decision-maker, but she never seemed to want to make up her mind about anything.

"At home I relax," she would say, but they all knew it had nothing to do with relaxation: She knew it was dangerous to think you could be a judge of everything everywhere, and she just didn't believe in treating her home like a courtroom. As she had told them more than once, "The problems that come up in court are much easier to solve than the problems that come up in a family."

So when Saundra looked to her, pleading for help, all Judge Leonard could do was look back at Saundra with a puzzled expression on her face, as if to say, "Are you asking *me?*"

Then Judge Leonard transferred her gaze to her husband, and opened her eyes wide at him, as if to say, "Your witness, counselor."

Their father nodded and took over. He said to Saundra, "It's all arranged, princess. Your sister's going to study dancing, she's going to study it at the American Ballet Center, and you're going to give her all the help you can."

Saundra stopped slumping. She sat up so straight in her chair all of a sudden that it looked to Lily as if someone had sent an electric shock through her seat. As her body jumped, Saundra began to speak, and the words poured out of her at great speed, with hardly a breath between sentences.

"How can I help her? She's just a beginner. She's not *even* a beginner. She hasn't even begun. She's a *pre*-beginner. I can't possibly help her. I don't have time. I have a class every day. I have rehearsal for my audition. I have my own private practice sessions for my audition. Besides, I'm not a teacher. I'm a dancer. How can I help her? Though God knows she's going to need help. But I can't help her. I have barely enough time to breathe. You know what it's like. If I take time out to help her, I'm not going to have enough time to practice to try to get into the company. And if I don't get into the company—"

"That's enough, sweetheart," said their father. "I didn't mean that kind of help. No one expects you to teach Lily how to dance. We just want you to help her get used to the school. She's never been to dancing school before. You're her sister. The least you can do—"

"No one helped *me*," said Saundra.

"That's true," said Judge Leonard.

Saundra looked at her mother with great relief, as if she finally had a friend at the table. Lily knew what it was like to feel as if no one in the whole world knew what you were talking about. She bet Saundra felt even more than relieved, she bet Saundra felt triumphant.

It certainly looked that way. Saundra sat up even straighter in her chair. She also jutted out her chin and cast her eyes haughtily about the table, looking from her mother to her father to Lily herself and then back to her mother. Lily almost expected her to get up from her chair and start dancing around the room.

"It *is* true," Saundra said. "So why should I—"

"Because she's your sister," their father interrupted.

"That doesn't make sense," Saundra said.

"It makes perfect sense to me," said their father.

"And to me," said their mother.

Saundra looked at Judge Leonard as if she had betrayed her.

Lily decided it was time for her to say something. What she really wanted to say was that it made sense to her too, that she wanted Saundra to help her a little bit at the beginning, because she was nervous about going to the school. But instead she decided to say, for one of the only times she could remember, that she agreed with Saundra. "It doesn't make sense to me either," she said.

"There, you see," said Saundra. "She doesn't even want my help, though—"

"You don't?" Lily's father said to her.

"—though God knows she needs it," Saundra went on.

"I agree," said their mother.

No one said anything for a few moments. Everyone looked at Judge Leonard.

Finally, their father, a puzzled expression on his face, said to their mother, "What the hell is going on here? Who do you agree *with?*"

Judge Leonard looked at her husband. Then she looked at her older daughter. And then she looked at her younger daughter. She opened her mouth to speak. Then she closed it. She seemed to be trying to make up her mind. "I agree . . ." she said and then stopped.

As if to help out her mother, Saundra said to her father, "You shouldn't swear at the table."

Now it was their father's turn to look puzzled. He squinted and opened his mouth halfway, as if trying to remember just what he had said.

Lily remembered. Last year, she knew, she would have said, in a singsong voice, "Daddy said a dirty word, Daddy said a dirty word." But now Lily felt too grown up to say such a thing. So she didn't say anything. Besides, she was waiting for her mother to explain just whom she *did* agree with. And besides that, she hadn't even noticed, until Saundra had made her remark, that her father had said "hell." It was curious, she thought. She hadn't even noticed it. Lily wondered if it was possible to have "dirty ears," the way some of her friends had "dirty mouths," because they used swear words all the time. If you had dirty ears, it meant you didn't even *hear* swear words when somebody said them.

Their father was still sitting there squinting, trying to remember what he had said.

"Hell," said Lily, to help him out.

"The same goes for you!" Saundra barked at her.

"Girls," said their father, "let's not have any—"

"I agree . . ." their mother began. Mr. Leonard fell silent. They all looked at Judge Leonard, who seemed finally willing to speak her mind. "I agree," she said again, "with *everyone*."

"The wisdom of Solomon," Mr. Leonard said and shook his head at the same time that he smiled at his wife with affection.

But Saundra was not smiling. She narrowed her eyes toward her mother and said, "Whose side are you on, anyway?"

Now it was Judge Leonard's turn to sit up straight in her chair. Lily imagined this was just how she did it in court when she was presiding at a case and someone said something that made her angry.

"There are no sides in this family, young lady. Do you understand me? No sides. We may not agree on everything—people often don't agree on things, even in families, *especially* in families—but we don't take sides. We try to do what is best for everyone. That's all. And in this case, what's best is for you to do everything you can to help out your sister in dancing school."

She stopped talking and looked around the table from person to person as if challenging everyone—anyone—to question her judgment.

Their father clapped his hands softly. "Case closed," he said.

Saundra looked down at her food, which she had hardly touched, and pushed her plate away from her. Then she got up without excusing herself and left the table, looking at no one, her chin up in the air, her toes spread so she looked as if she had just finished a dance and were leaving the stage and didn't give a hoot that no one was applauding her.

Lily knew she had just won something—her parents had agreed that Saundra must help her. But she didn't feel good. She felt confused. She didn't want to go to dancing school. But if she had to go, she wanted Saundra to help her, at least in the beginning, because she'd never been to dancing school, and she was scared. So she was sad and glad at the same time. Sometimes it was so hard to make up your mind about things. Sometimes she felt she understood perfectly why her mother needed some time off from telling the world what was right and what was wrong.

·6·
Numb Legs

Saundra and Lily took the bus down Central Park West, got off at 66th Street, and walked west toward Lincoln Center. The American Ballet Center was on Broadway, right across from Lincoln Center. Almost every night of the year, at about seven thirty, the street around Lincoln Center became filled with people walking from all directions toward the wide, open plaza, with the gushing, shooting fountain in its center that stood surrounded by the Lincoln Center buildings.

Lily had always loved it there, in the plaza. The few times she had gone with her parents to a concert in Avery Fisher Hall, an opera in the Metropolitan Opera House, or a ballet in the New York State Theater she had tried to make them stay outside by the fountain until the last possible moment. She knew that when she was old enough to stay out by herself in New York, especially at night, she would come to Lincoln Center and sit on the rim of the fountain and listen to the water and be sprinkled by it and watch all the people gathering from all directions on their way to one of the buildings. And at eight o'clock, when all the programs began, the plaza would be nearly empty, and still Lily would sit by the fountain, letting everyone else go off to their assigned seats while she sat alone, happy and peaceful and full of her own thoughts of anything in the world she wanted to think about. Then she would walk home, to read a book or go to sleep. And maybe she would stop for a glass of wine on the way—but that wouldn't happen until she was old enough; that wouldn't happen for almost ten years.

Today Lily knew she'd see Lincoln Center only from a distance, because they would reach Broadway before they would reach Lincoln Center, and they'd turn left, downtown, on Broadway and walk until they reached the American Ballet Center.

During the bus ride, Lily pictured Lincoln Center and wished that she could go and sit by the fountain and never set foot in the American Ballet Center.

She didn't want to dance. She hated the whole idea. She was nervous and frightened and lonely.

It didn't help her loneliness to have Saundra with her. Saundra didn't say a word to her for nearly the whole bus ride. Saundra just sat there next to her, sitting up so straight that Lily felt like a midget. Saundra had her haughtiest look on her face, and she stared ahead, looking out the window as they passed building after building on their way down Central Park West.

Lily, on the other hand, couldn't keep her eyes steady. They darted about the bus, looking from passenger to passenger, and, as usual, she wondered where everyone was going. She always figured that at least one person on any particular bus was going to the dentist, and that person was always the unhappiest person. She always tried to pick out just who it might be. She also tried to pick out who the happiest person was. The happiest person was probably going to a birthday party, or was having her own birthday party later that very day. The trouble with picking out the happiest person was that you couldn't always judge by who was smiling or laughing the most, particularly because there was usually a drunk sitting at the back of every bus, laughing away at nothing in particular, talking to himself, and sometimes even slapping his thigh in glee, and smiling with a crazy grin at anyone who made the mistake of looking his way and catching his eye. So drunk people didn't count.

Today Lily couldn't find anyone who seemed to be all that happy. She couldn't even find anybody drunk. And as for the unhappiest person on the bus, she didn't care if anybody was going to the dentist or to get a shot at the doctor's office or to visit a sick relative who might be dying.

Lily knew that no matter where anyone else was going, it was she herself who was the unhappiest person on the bus. For one thing, now that the day of her first dancing lesson had arrived, she knew she didn't want to go to it at all. And for another, her sister was not helping her but was making matters worse by ignoring her completely.

Lily felt totally alone. Even as she looked around the bus at all the people, she felt alone, and it didn't help that no one looked back at her. She felt invisible, invisible and alone.

Saundra, who was looking at no one, was getting all the attention. Saundra sat there, straight and haughty, staring out the window, and nearly everyone on the bus was looking at *her*. As Lily could see, some of them just sat there and stared at Saundra. But others were more shy and darted their eyes at Saundra, let them rest for a moment on her face or her hair or her straight shoulders or her small breasts that stood out in her leotard. But only for a moment; then those shy people would look down to the floor for another moment before looking up again at Saundra.

Saundra seemed to notice none of it. As the blocks went by, she just stared out the window, her eyes hardly blinking as they looked slightly down because of the way she held her head, chin up. And yet, Lily had a feeling that Saundra knew very well that everyone was looking at her. There was no way to tell for sure. But Lily suspected that Saundra was putting on a show.

It made her feel all the more alone. Here she was, going off to her first ballet class, accompanied for the ride at least by her big sister, who was already a champion dancer and knew everything about dancing and dance classes that Lily didn't know. Lily felt stupid beside her. Lily felt small beside her. Lily felt ugly beside her. And, worst, Lily felt invisible beside her.

Lily was the one who looked all over the bus, at everyone, trying to see people and to figure out who they were and what they were doing and how they were feeling. Lily was the one who was trying to reach out.

And Saundra was the one who looked at no one, not even her own sister. Saundra was the one who looked only at the street. Or perhaps, Lily thought, Saundra was trying to see her own reflection in the opposite window.

It was Saundra who should have been invisible. It didn't seem right that the way to make people look at you was not to look at them. But maybe it was.

Lily sat up straight, stuck her chin into the air, lowered her eyes, and stared out the window.

It's working, she thought. It's working. People are looking at me.

It was true. The people sitting opposite her were looking at her. But they were laughing.

Lily didn't know why they were laughing at her until she felt Saundra's hand on her legs, pushing them down.

Oh, both her legs were sticking straight out! She hadn't even known it. But when she'd straightened her body, she'd also lifted her legs and stuck them straight out in front of her, not only blocking the aisle but also making herself look like a stiff doll whose knees refused to bend.

"You look ridiculous," Saundra whispered, as she made Lily aware of her legs by pushing them down.

Lily wanted to cry. She wanted to run from the bus and go sit by the fountain in Lincoln Center or hide in Central Park until the time her class was supposed to be over. She felt miserable, embarrassed and clumsy.

But then Saundra said, "Relax, Lily," and her voice was kind. Lily did relax, or tried to. She let her whole body slump, she no longer tried to sit like Saundra, and if she'd dared, she would have let her head fall against her sister's arm. But she didn't dare. Still, Saundra had told her to relax. Saundra had helped her. Maybe, Lily thought, Saundra really would help her learn how to dance.

But, as the two of them walked down 66th Street, Saundra said nothing to her. As usual, she walked with such long strides that Lily nearly had to run to keep up, and even then she was always a step behind.

Saundra carried all her dance things in a canvas shoulder bag that had her initials printed on it in big, bold letters: SRL. As she walked, the bag swung back and forth and several times nearly clipped Lily on the nose.

Lily had her brand-new black leotard, black tights, and black dance slippers in her Capezio bag, which hung from her wrist by its strings. Lily hated the plastic Capezio bag. For one thing, it said Capezio, and Capezio meant dance, and at this moment Lily hated dancing more than anything else in the world. For another, the Capezio bag reminded her of all the dozens of Capezio bags she'd been living with for years, in her and Saundra's bedroom, where the bags lay around stuffed with Saundra's smelly things. And for another, her Capezio bag wasn't nearly as pretty as Saundra's canvas bag, with its beautiful beige fabric and large purple letters.

Everything was wrong. Lily wanted to turn around and run back home. If she did, Saundra probably wouldn't even notice, since she was walking ahead of Lily and never looked back. But if she did, how would she be able to face her mother and father? And for how many years would Saundra tease her? And what would she do with her brand-new leotard and tights and dance slippers?

Lily was caught. There was no turning back now.

She was going to her beginner's class—and how embarrassing *that* was, compared with Saundra's advanced class—at the American Ballet Center, and there was nothing she could do to avoid it.

Unless she fell down and broke her leg or something!

She stopped walking. Sure enough, Saundra didn't notice and kept right on going.

Lily sat down on the sidewalk and put her bag neatly beside her and then lay down and stuck one leg up in the air.

"Saundra!" she called.

Saundra was already so far away that she didn't even hear her.

"Saundra!" she screamed. "Saundra!"

This time Saundra heard and turned slowly around. She looked at Lily lying there on the ground with her leg stuck up in the air, but she didn't come toward her, she only put her hand on her hip and nodded her head.

"What are you doing?" she asked.

"I think I hurt my leg," she shouted.

"Which one?"

Lily thought for a moment. "This one," she said, shaking the one that was stuck up in the air.

"Which one?" Saundra asked again.

"This one," said Lily again, shaking it even harder.

"Oh, that one," said Saundra. "Are you sure it's that one and not the other one?"

"Of course I'm sure."

"Come off it, Lily."

"What do you mean?"

"Get up, Lily!"

"I can't. I think I broke my leg."

"The one sticking up in the air? The one you were wiggling around? Really, Lily, you must think I'm an idiot."

"I will think you're an idiot if you don't . . ." Lily stopped. What did she want Saundra to do? What if Saundra called a doctor? Or their parents? She couldn't think of anything to say. So she said, without thinking, "Maybe it's the other leg."

"The other leg?" Saundra looked up in the air and shook her head impatiently.

"They're both so numb," Lily said, now thinking fast to try to get herself out of this fix. "Maybe it's neither leg. Maybe they're not really broken. They're both so numb. I can't feel anything in either one."

"Oh," said Saundra. "You have a case of numb legs."

"I think so," said Lily.

"*You're* the idiot!" screamed Saundra. "There's no such thing as numb legs!"

"There isn't?" said Lily.

"Numb legs!" exclaimed Saundra. "My God! Numb legs!"

"Well," said Lily, "when I get pins and needles—you know, when my legs fall asleep—they *feel* numb. *That's* a case of numb legs."

"Oh, sure," said Saundra. "Just the thing to get when you're walking along the street."

"Oh," said Lily, because she couldn't think of anything else to say.

Finally Saundra walked toward her. When she reached her, she said, "We're going to be late. Get up. I'm responsible for you, so you've got to come to class. As you know very well, *I* don't want you at my school. And if *you* don't want to go—if you'll go to such lengths as this, pretending you have broken legs and numb legs—then all you have to do is tell Mom and Dad after your class that you never want to go again. Okay? Do you understand? You have to go to this class, but you don't have to go to any more classes. So get up now, Lily, and come with me. But as soon as we get home, you'll tell Mom and Dad that you tried out dancing school and you've decided you aren't going back. Okay? You know they'll listen to you. You can even cry if you want. Today you try it, and that will be enough to satisfy them. All you have to take is one class, and then you'll never have to take another one as long as you live. Okay? Do you understand?"

"Yes," said Lily.

"So we have a deal?" asked Saundra.

"I don't know," said Lily.

"Don't worry," Saundra said, trying to smile. All Saundra could ever do was *try* to smile. Someone must have told her once that ballerinas don't smile. Saundra didn't know how to smile. She just sort of made the corners of her mouth wink up into her cheeks. Her eyes didn't change at all. Saundra's smile made her face look as if it were made of wax. It was scary.

"Really," she went on. "Don't worry. They won't be mad at you. The main thing is that you gave it a try. Come on. You'll give it a try today, and you'll never have to do it again. What a good idea."

Saundra reached down and held her hand out to Lily.

Lily couldn't believe it. Saundra was actually helping her get up! It must be part of the deal.

Lily took her sister's hand and felt Saundra pull her up in one swift motion. Strong. Lily had never realized it. Saundra was really strong. It must have come from her dancing. Saundra looked so thin, and yet she was so strong. Lily had never thought about that part of dancing. It could make you strong. Maybe it could even make you thin. Maybe Saundra herself would have been round, just like Lily, if it weren't for dancing. After all, they were sisters. Maybe Lily could get strong from dancing. Maybe she could even learn to look haughty like Saundra, not that she'd ever want to, except at certain moments when other snotty people were bothering her. Maybe, deep down, she and Saundra were just the same, except that Saundra had been dancing for years and Lily had never danced before.

"How old were you when you started dancing?"

Lily asked her as they started to walk again toward the school.

"Nine," said Saundra.

"Nine!" said Lily.

"Yes," said Saundra. "Why?"

"*I'm* nine," said Lily.

"Oh," said Saundra. "What does that have to do with it?"

"It means that I—never mind," said Lily, thinking better of telling Saundra that maybe when she, Lily, had been dancing for five or six years, she would be as good as Saundra was now. Even better.

"Do you want me to carry you?" Saundra asked.

"Carry me! Into school?"

"Well, if you have numb legs . . ."

"The feeling is coming back to them," Lily said.

"Lucky for you."

"I know it."

"Now you'll be able to dance up a storm," said Saundra, still teasing.

And blow you right over, thought Lily, though she said nothing and started to limp a little so Saundra might wonder, just might wonder, if maybe she really did have a case of numb legs.

·7·

The Dressing Room

"This is where we change," said Saundra, leading Lily into an enormous ugly room filled with girls of all ages, who were making so much noise that Lily wanted to put her hands over her ears. It was quite frightening. Lily felt glad for once that she had Saundra with her. What if she were all alone! She didn't know anybody. She wouldn't know what to do. She would be lost.

Having Saundra made all the difference. Saundra had been coming here for over five years. Saundra was one of the best dancers in the school. Saundra knew exactly what to do and how to do it. It was such a relief. For the first time Lily was glad, really glad, that her parents had insisted that Saundra help her and that she herself had not been taken seriously when she'd said at the dinner table that it didn't make sense for Saundra to help her. Now that she was here, in this big room whose every inch seemed to be taken up by strange girls and all their clothes and bags and equipment, it made perfect sense: an older sister should help a younger sister.

Lily took Saundra's hand as they started to walk through the rooms.

"What are you doing?" said Saundra.

"What do you mean?"

"What are you doing with my hand?"

"I don't know," said Lily.

"Let go of it," said Saundra. "You can't hold my hand in here."

"Why not?" asked Lily, still holding on.

"You're not a baby," whispered Saundra, trying to pull her hand away. "Let go."

Lily gripped Saundra's hand as hard as she could. "No," she said.

"Come *on*, Lily. Let *go*," Saundra insisted.

They were now in the middle of the room. Other girls were looking at them. Lily suddenly felt embarrassed that she was holding on to her sister's hand, but she just couldn't make herself let go.

"Hi, Saundra," said one girl.

"Hi, Saundra," said someone else.

"Saundra's here," said yet another, though Lily couldn't see that she was saying it to anyone in particular. But as soon as she'd said it, girls all over the

room turned from what they were doing—putting on
their tights and leotards, slipping on their shoes, fixing
their hair and makeup—to look at Saundra and say
"Hello" or "How are you?" or "What's going on?" or
"Who's that?"

That, Lily realized, was herself.

Lily waited for Saundra to tell all these people who
she was, but Saundra said nothing, not a word, not even
"hello" to answer all the greetings. Saundra merely
walked straight and tall and haughty through the room,
her hand limp in Lily's hand, which gripped her sister's
hand with all her might.

"You're not very courteous," Lily whispered.

"What do you mean?"

"You didn't say hello to anybody."

"I never do," said Saundra. "Now let go of my
hand."

"You don't even say hello?" asked Lily, still holding
on.

"They aren't my friends," said Saundra. "They
pretend to be, but they aren't."

"Well, what are they then? They seem to be your
friends. They seem to like you."

"They're my enemies."

"What?"

"My enemies," said Saundra, pointing with her free
hand to a small space on a bench. "Sit there," she said.

Lily didn't sit. She stood next to her sister and
continued to grip her hand.

"All of them?" she asked. "All of them are your enemies?"

"Not all of them," said Saundra. "Some of them just want to be my friend because I'm such a good dancer. They think *they'll* seem like better dancers if I'm friendly to them. But the rest are my enemies."

"Why?" asked Lily. "Do they want to kill you or something?"

"They want to beat me."

"Beat you *up?*" asked Lily, who had a picture in her mind of a group of girls surrounding Saundra and hitting her with their fists.

"Beat me *out*," said Saundra.

"Out?" said Lily.

"For the company," Saundra answered.

"Oh," said Lily, nodding. Then she realized she still didn't understand. She hated to be ignorant in front of Saundra, but she found herself asking: "What does that mean?"

"I thought you knew. There's going to be one open place for a female dancer in the second company. It's going to be filled by the end of the summer, in time for rehearsals for the fall season. And whoever gets it will dance with the second company beginning with the fall season. And I want it. But so do all the other girls. That's why they're not my friends."

"Gee," said Lily. "You'll be on stage and everything. People will come every night and watch you, huh? You'll get to take bows and everything."

"I'll get to dance with the company," said Saundra.

"That's terrific, Saundra," said Lily. "Maybe I can come and watch you."

"You have to have a ticket," said Saundra.

"I'll save up," said Lily.

"You better start now," said Saundra. "The tickets cost a lot."

"Do you get some of the money?"

"Sure," said Saundra. "When you're part of the company, you get paid. You're a professional."

"Wow!" said Lily. "A professional! Just like Chris Evert."

"She's a tennis player, silly."

"I know," said Lily. "But she's a *professional*. Dad explained to me that professional means you get paid. And amateur means you don't get paid. It means you do something just because you love to do it, not because you get paid."

"I don't want to be an amateur," said Saundra.

"Don't you love to dance?" asked Lily.

"I never think about it that way," Saundra answered.

"You don't?" Lily was surprised. She had always thought that Saundra danced every day and lived her whole life for dancing because she loved it. "How come?"

"It hurts too much."

"It *hurts?*"

"Yes, it hurts. You'll see. Today may be your only

lesson—remember that we have a deal, remember that you're going to quit after today. So today will be your only lesson. But even one day, one lesson, is going to hurt. You'll see."

"I will?"

"Yes."

"It's going to hurt?"

"Yes."

"How much?"

"You'll see."

Lily gripped Saundra's hand even harder. "I think my legs are getting numb again," she said.

She meant it to be funny and to take her mind off this business about hurting, but as she said it, she actually began to sense that her legs were getting weaker, that she was losing her feeling in them. Of course that was ridiculous. But it was like the feeling you get when something frightens you—a loud noise in the street, a scary shadow on the wall at night; your body tingles, almost like pins and needles, and you tremble and begin to lose the feeling in your limbs.

"If your legs are numb, then sit down," said Saundra, pulling her hand out of Lily's grasp and pointing again to the space on the bench. Lily realized too late that she'd given Saundra the right excuse to take her hand away. Slowly, Lily, feeling her legs still trembling, sat down.

"And don't just think about your legs," said Saundra, as she began to walk away. "Worry about your feet." And with that, she pointed at the feet of the girl next to Lily and disappeared into the crowd of girls, who once again started to greet her and to ask who that was who had been holding her hand.

Lily looked at the girl's feet. She couldn't believe her eyes.

Blood! There was blood on both her feet, all over the toes. The girl seemed hardly to notice. She just sat there staring off into space and wiped at the blood with her tights, which she had taken off and rolled up so that they were like a towel. They were white tights, and where the blood touched them, they turned pink.

Lily looked at the blood and the tights, she couldn't take her eyes from them. When the blood was almost all removed from the girl's toes, Lily realized that her toes still looked strange, almost as if they still had blood on them, or dried beneath the nails. Her toes were black. Ugly feet, thought Lily, remembering what her father had said. Ugly feet.

"What are you looking at?" said the girl, who was around Saundra's age.

Lily almost jumped from the bench.

"What are you looking at?" the girl said again.

"Nothing," said Lily.

"Are you looking at my feet?"

"I don't know," said Lily.

"You were," said the girl.

"I guess so," said Lily.

"Well, don't," said the girl. "I don't appreciate it."

She sounded a lot like Saundra. Maybe Saundra wasn't really snotty. Not deep down. Maybe she just got that way from coming to the American Ballet Center. Maybe all dancers got snotty.

Lily turned away. She felt like crying. She didn't want to dance. Not even once. The only thing that gave her hope was the deal Saundra said they had. If she went along with it, she would go to class today, and then she would quit. Being a dancer was terrible. She hadn't had even one lesson, and she knew that being a dancer was terrible. People were snotty. Not only that: their feet got bloody too. Their feet got so hurt that blood flowed out of them.

"Hey," said the girl. "I'm sorry."

"What?" said Lily. She could hardly believe her ears.

"Are you new?" the girl asked her.

Lily turned to her. She could hardly believe her eyes. The girl was speaking to her from inside her leotard, which had snaps at the bottom and which the girl was pulling off over her head. She had nothing on underneath. She was naked. Her stomach and breasts and everything showed. Lily closed her eyes.

"Are you new?" the girl asked again.

"Not so," said Lily, knowing what the girl meant but ashamed to admit that this was her first lesson. If the girl persisted, Lily was going to say that she was certainly not new, she was nine.

"Then why were you looking at my feet?"

"I felt sorry for them." Slowly Lily opened her eyes, trying not to look at the girl's feet. She peeked at the rest of the girl and was relieved to see that she had on another leotard now and was pulling on a pair of corduroys.

"For my feet?" the girl asked.

"Sure."

"What about yours?"

"Mine?" said Lily, not knowing what to say. She thought her feet were fine, even if the toes were a little stubby. But maybe around here they were *too* fine; maybe around here you were nowhere if you didn't have bloody, ugly feet.

"Yeah," said the girl. "Yours bleed?"

"Nope," said Lily.

"Don't you go on point?"

"What?"

"Point," said the girl.

"At what?"

"Ha ha," said the girl. "A regular little joker."

"I don't know what you mean," Lily admitted.

"You new?" asked the girl for the third time.

"I guess so," Lily confessed now.

"Why didn't you say so in the first place?" she asked. But before Lily could answer, she went on: "Oh, never mind. I know it's hard to admit you're stupid about something. Want a piece of gum?" She held out a pack.

"No thanks."

The girl took out two sticks of gum, peeled the paper from them, and stuck them both into her mouth. Lily looked around—and noticed that practically everyone was chewing gum, or at least all the older girls were, the ones who looked the most haughty, the most like real dancers. Some of them were putting on their leotards, some of them were taking off their leotards, most of them were at least partly naked, and nearly all of them were chewing away. It looked strange to see such beautiful girls, with such stuck-out chins and long necks, chewing away on big wads of gum.

"Utsurname?" said the girl.

"What?"

The girl moved the gum around in her mouth. "What's your name?"

"Oh," said Lily. "Lily Leonard."

"Are you related to Saundra Leonard?"

"I'm her sister."

"Her sister! Oh, wow. Really? Wow. She's really good. She's one of the best dancers here. If you turn out to be only half as good as she is . . . She might get into the second company. But of course you already know that."

Lily nodded and didn't admit that she hadn't known very much at all about Saundra's getting into the company until today.

"Do you think she can beat out Meredith Meredith?" the girl asked.

"Who?"

"Meredith Meredith."

"Is that someone's name?"

"You're Saundra Leonard's sister, and you've never heard of Meredith Meredith?"

"I don't think so," said Lily.

"Well, she's your sister's main competition for the place in the company. Five girls have been picked to audition, but everyone says that it's really between your sister and Meredith Meredith. I can't believe you've never heard of her."

"My sister doesn't take the office home with her," Lily said, using an expression she had often heard her father use about himself to explain why he was able to relax in the evenings.

"What office?" asked the girl, with a perplexed look on her face. But before Lily could explain, the girl bent to stuff her dance clothes in her bag, stood straight up, and said, "You're kind of strange. Good luck anyway. Tell your sister you talked to me. Tell her I think she's a real neat dancer. Okay?"

"Okay," said Lily, but the girl was already walking away. "What's your name?" Lily asked, but the girl, who was swallowed up in the noise made by all the other girls, couldn't hear her. Anyway, Lily wouldn't have told Saundra even if she knew the girl's name.

Saundra had enough of a swelled head. There was no use telling her that perfect strangers thought she was so neat.

Lily looked at the clock on the wall and realized she had to hurry if she wasn't going to be late for her class. Other classes must be ending, because the room was getting more and more crowded; a steady stream of sweaty girls was pouring in through the door. It was getting noisier and noisier and hotter and hotter and smellier and smellier.

She took her dance clothes out of her Capezio bag and put them down beside her on the bench. Feeling strange, she took off her sneakers and then her pants. With her sweatshirt pulled down as far as it would go to cover her underpants, she pulled on her tights, without standing up but leaning forward at just the right moment to get them over her bottom. Then she bent forward and put her legs into her leotard and stood up and pulled the leotard right up under her sweatshirt. She freed her arms from the sweatshirt and, still keeping it on, maneuvered her arms into the armholes of the leotard and, reaching into her sweatshirt, hitched the straps up over her shoulders. Only then did she remove the sweatshirt, pulling it up over her head.

When it was off, she noticed that another girl had sat down in the tiny space on the bench next to her.

"Some people," the girl said, "will do anything to

keep other people from seeing them naked." And with that, the girl jumped up, let her pants drop, stepped out of them, took off her underpants, took off her sweater, took off her bra, stood there completely naked and twirled around on one foot, shouting, "I'm beautiful! I'm beautiful!"

While another girl across the room shouted at the naked girl, "You're fat! You're fat!" Lily hurriedly pulled on her dance slippers, gathered up her street clothes, and jumped up from the bench.

There wasn't a hanger to be found, so, like so many other girls, she simply put her clothes and sneakers on top of her bag and placed the whole thing against the wall. She hoped no one would steal her things. She doubted anyone would, since she hadn't seen anyone who dressed quite like her.

As she walked out to look for her class, she noticed dozens of girls trying to see themselves in the one small mirror. Some of them were putting their hair up in buns, and others were putting on all sorts of makeup.

Lily knew she was too young for makeup and that it was hopeless for her to try to make a bun.

Blocking the doorway were some older girls who had just come from class. They were sweating and chewing gum and drinking diet soda from cans. Over their heads was a sign: NO FOOD OR DRINK IN THIS DRESSING ROOM.

"Excuse me," said Lily.

"Why? What did you do?" asked one of the girls.

None of them had moved an inch, so they were still blocking the doorway.

"Excuse me, please," said Lily again.

"Excuse you for what?" asked the same girl.

"Maybe she farted," said a very pretty girl, taking her nose between her forefinger and thumb and starting to laugh.

Two other girls also laughed.

Another girl said, "Don't be gross."

"Oh, shut up, Hilary," said the girl who was holding her nose.

"Up yours, Meredith," said the girl named Hilary. "Here," she said to Lily and stepped aside so Lily could get through.

Lily walked away, turning around only once to try to find Saundra, to ask her where the beginners' class was and to tell her that she knew all about Meredith Meredith and their competition for the place in the company, and that she thought she had just met Meredith Meredith, who had a filthy mouth. But Saundra wasn't there. Saundra had disappeared. Or at least Lily couldn't find her. So she walked away by herself, looking for the class for beginners.

She felt funny-looking and clumsy among so many beautiful girls who obviously had been dancing for years. But what she couldn't figure out was why so many of them looked so pretty and delicate and strong and graceful and yet were so gross, as the girl Hilary had said; gross with gum chewing and slurping soda out of cans and their toilet jokes and their meanness to little kids like her. She had always thought dancers were supposed to be like magic, doing things that made you believe the impossible. Now she was beginning to think that it was all one big trick.

·8·
Leaps and Bounds

When Lily found her classroom, she was late. The teacher was already talking to the class. But when Lily entered, the teacher stopped talking. She was a short woman dressed, like Lily, all in black. Lily noticed this, and so, apparently, did the teacher, who looked Lily up and down as Lily walked into the room, holding her breath and wondering where she should stand.

"Look at your hair," said the woman.

Lily froze. The rest of the class started to snicker and laugh.

"Tie it up next time. You can't dance if your body goes in one direction and your hair goes in the other."

The class laughed again.

"And be on time next time," said the teacher.

Lily stood stock still. She wanted to cry. She also wanted to leap up in the air and fly around the room like the greatest ballerina who had ever lived, fly around the room without her feet ever touching the floor, so the teacher and all the students would hold their breath and then gasp and then cheer and cheer.

"Go stand over there," said the teacher, pointing to the back of the room.

Her legs felt really numb now, but Lily moved them, one after the other, and she made it to her place.

"Now, as I was saying," said the teacher. "What we must learn is *technique*. Technique! Without technique, none of you will ever be a dancer. Dance is first of all technique. Technique, technique, technique! There is nothing you can do in dance without technique. There is no step, no leap, no arabesque, no *écart*, otherwise known as a split, no *cabriole*, no *ballon*, no anything—there is nothing that can be mastered without technique. Am I understood?"

No one said anything. A few of the girls nodded. There were about thirty in all, with just two boys that Lily could see, one of them fat and dressed in tights and a football shirt, which made him look even fatter, and the other a little guy with black hair and a green leotard who looked like a small prince in a storybook.

"Technique is tedious," the teacher went on. "To learn technique is to practice the same thing over and over and over. It is to practice something until you are so tired of it that you forget you are even practicing, and what you are practicing becomes part of your body. Some of you may wonder why dancers carry their bodies as if they were dancing even when they are not dancing, even when they are merely walking down the street or sleeping in their beds. The reason is that they have *absorbed* technique. They have become technique, and technique has become them. They are no longer normal human beings. They are *dance*. And that is why they are so beautiful. They are dance. So they are beautiful. Am I understood?"

Lily nodded. So did a few of the others.

The teacher said, "My name is Miss Witt. I have been teaching dance for twenty years, and I have seen no students who were beautiful when they came to me and very few students who were beautiful when they left me. I expect nothing different from you. None of you is beautiful now, let me tell you. Very few of you—perhaps none of you—will be beautiful when you leave me. And the reason: because no matter what I tell you, you will not learn technique, you will not see the point of it, you will become bored. 'Teach us to dance, Miss Witt,' you will say, 'teach us to fly, to twirl, to bend like a swan. Teach us to *dance*.' All along, I shall be teaching you technique. And you will not realize, no matter what I tell you now, that by teaching you technique, I am teaching you to dance. So you will become bored, and leave me. You will not learn technique. And thus you will not learn to dance.

And thus you will never be beautiful. Am I understood?"

She didn't wait for a reaction. "To the *barre*, then!" she shouted, and motioned with her hand for the class to line up at the long pole that was fastened to one of the walls. The class scurried to the *barre*.

Miss Witt sat down on a stool that was near the opposite wall, which was completely covered with a mirror. Next to her stood a younger woman in tights and a leotard. Miss Witt was talking to her while the class lined up. At one side of the room a man sat at a piano, drinking coffee from a plastic cup and reading a magazine that was propped up on the piano keys.

"This is Mrs. Howell," said Miss Witt, indicating the woman by her side. "She is my assistant. I am here to teach you. She is here to show you what I am teaching you. She is also here to help you. If she touches you, and tries to move your body, relax and let her move you. She knows your body better than you do. Become putty in her hands, and she'll make you pretty putty." Miss Witt made a noise that sounded as if she were choking. Lily looked at her and realized that she was smiling. The choking noise was Miss Witt's way of laughing. But no one got the joke. "Pretty putty," Miss Witt said again, and started to choke again.

But when no one else laughed this time either, Miss Witt suddenly got a fierce look on her face and screamed, "First position!"

Some of the students immediately gripped the *barre* and moved their feet so that their toes pointed in opposite directions, with their heels touching. The rest tried to see what the others were doing.

"Don't look at *them!*" shouted Miss Witt. "If you don't know the position, look at Mrs. Howell."

Mrs. Howell was standing halfway between Miss Witt and the students and was in first position.

Lily put her heels together and then swiveled her feet out so that her toes began to separate. She kept moving them until they went as far as she could make them go. But they still formed only a V shape, not the straight line that Mrs. Howell was demonstrating.

"More! More!" shouted Miss Witt, to all those students whose feet looked like Lily's.

Lily strained to move her feet even farther apart. Finally she got them into a straight line. Her knees hurt a little, but at least her feet were pointing in opposite directions.

"Keep your heels *together!*" screamed Miss Witt. "Heels together. You, Curly, put your heels together." Lily realized with a shock that Miss Witt was talking to *her*. She looked down and saw that while her toes were indeed pointing in opposite directions, her heels weren't touching. She had forgotten to keep her heels together. "Go help Curly, Mrs. Howell. The rest of you, second position!"

Mrs. Howell came over to Lily and placed a gentle hand on each of her feet and pulled her heels together while keeping both feet in a straight line, pointing out. "Good," she said, and patted Lily's thigh as she rose and walked back to her place between Miss Witt and the students. Once there, Mrs. Howell demonstrated second position: both feet in the same line as for first position but with a space between them.

Lily kept her feet pointed in opposite directions and separated them. It felt easier to do this than to stand in first position.

"Knees straight!" shouted Miss Witt. Many of the girls had bent their legs. But Lily hadn't. Her knees were locked in position. She stood straight, in second position, and felt proud.

"Now, third position!" screamed Miss Witt. "Watch Mrs. Howell."

Third position was the hardest one yet. You had to put one foot in front of the other, pointing in opposite directions, with the heel of the front foot touching the middle of the other foot.

At first Lily had trouble keeping her balance, but finally she managed to stand still. All the while, she kept her knees straight.

Some of the students had trouble with this position. The fat boy in the football shirt tripped as he was moving his feet and fell to the floor. Many of the other students laughed when they saw him lying on the floor. He looked up at the sound of the laughter, and his face went from pale to red, right before their eyes.

That made them laugh more. The boy lay on the floor and covered his face with his arms.

Lily didn't laugh. She felt sorry for him. She was very worried that when he finally took his arms from around his face, he would be crying and tears would be streaming down his face. As he lay there, his body shook. Lily almost felt like crying herself, as she watched him on the floor, his chubby sides shaking through his shirt.

"Get him off the floor, Mrs. Howell," ordered Miss Witt.

It was an unnecessary command, for Mrs. Howell had already been on her way to help the boy. It also seemed cruel to Lily, since it made absolutely everybody stare at the poor boy on the floor and started more people laughing.

Mrs. Howell bent over the boy and put her hands on both his arms, which remained over his face. His body still shook. He resisted Mrs. Howell's attempts to separate his arms from his head. The more he resisted, the more the class laughed.

Lily felt like telling everyone to shut up. She wondered why Miss Witt didn't go on and do some more in third position or move on to the next position, if there was another one. By stopping the whole class and making everyone look at the boy on the floor, she was only making him more miserable. Lily had an image of him lying there during the whole class, never removing his arms, and his parents coming to get him and picking him up and carrying him away with his arms still held tightly across his face so no one would see his red eyes and the tears streaming down his face. Lily was embarrassed for him. It was all so cruel.

Finally Mrs. Howell leaned over even farther and started to say something to the boy. She was aiming at his ear, though obviously she couldn't see his ear because his arms were covering both his ears. So she spoke more or less to his elbow, and at the same time she had her hands on each of his arms and kept trying to separate them from his head.

Lily couldn't hear what Mrs. Howell was saying—no one could, she was sure—but she imagined it was something soothing and nice. It made Lily feel good to imagine that Mrs. Howell was telling the boy that if he just got up and started to dance, he would fly around the room in great leaps and bounds and astound all the rest of the class, Miss Witt included. But Lily knew that Mrs. Howell wasn't saying that. The boy was fat. The boy was clumsy. He was so clumsy that he fell down doing third position, which even she could do without all that much trouble, and keeping her knees straight too. Mrs. Howell wouldn't tell him he could dance like a gazelle when in truth he floundered around like a hippopotamus in the mud.

So then Lily imagined that Mrs. Howell was telling the boy that he could get up and go right home, that he didn't have to stay for the rest of the class and do all the rest of the positions and fall down that many more times. That would be nice to tell the boy. He'd be sure to get up if he knew he didn't have to stay and listen to the other students laugh at him every time he tried something new.

But the more Mrs. Howell talked to him and tried to pull his arms from his head, the more the boy shook, and the more he shook, the more the class laughed.

"That's enough!" screamed Miss Witt. "I won't have my class disrupted in this way!" And with that, she strode over to the boy and Mrs. Howell, tapped Mrs. Howell on the shoulder and motioned for her to rise, and yelled at the boy, "Get up this instant!"

The boy's body started to shake more than ever before, it shook so much it almost started to bounce around right there on the floor. The class laughed even harder.

"Enough!" bellowed Miss Witt. "If you don't get up this instant, you will leave my class!"

Suddenly the boy turned over onto his back, removed his arms from around his head, stuck them out to the sides, and let out the loudest howl Lily had ever heard. He howled and howled and shook and shook, and tears streamed down his face.

But everyone realized all at once that the boy wasn't crying. The boy was laughing. Laughing!

All the while he had been lying there laughing! He'd

been so embarrassed by his laughter that he'd tried to hide it. The more everyone else had laughed, the more the boy had laughed.

And now that everyone saw that *he* was laughing, they all began to laugh. Even Lily.

She was terribly relieved. The boy had been laughing. Not crying. Laughing. So she laughed too.

But the more she laughed, the more she began to feel it was just as sad that the boy had been laughing as it would have been if he'd been crying. There was nothing really funny about falling down in the middle of a class filled with other kids. The boy couldn't really have thought it was so funny. But he laughed anyway. Maybe laughing was his way of crying. It certainly looked the same in a lot of ways.

Lily stopped laughing and wished everyone else would too. But they didn't.

So Lily walked over to Mrs. Howell, who was maybe the only other person not laughing, and she asked her in a loud voice, "Will you please show me third position again?"

"Of course," said Mrs. Howell, putting her hand on Lily's shoulder and leading her back to her place at the *barre*. She demonstrated third position once again for Lily, who watched her and then took the position herself.

A number of other students started to watch the two of them, and they too tried out third position again. Pretty soon most of the class was back in third position, and they stopped laughing as they started to plant their feet and try to keep their balance.

Miss Witt walked away from the fat boy and went to her stool. As soon as she had turned her back on the boy, he got to his feet, shook his body as if his clothes had gotten dusty from the floor, leaned against the *barre* for balance, and moved his own feet into third position, which he managed to assume as long as he had the *barre* for support, and stood there shaking a bit but still maintaining, proudly, the same position that last time had made him flop to the floor. He had an enormous grin on his rosy face. Lily could imagine him thinking to himself that it wouldn't be long before he'd be flying around the room in leaps and bounds.

Mrs. Howell started to walk away from Lily to go help other members of the class. But as she was walking away, she turned back to look at Lily and said, "Thank you."

Lily said nothing. She was concentrating too hard on holding third position. But in her mind she was saying, "On to fourth position! . . . if there is one."

Meredith Meredith

By the time she returned to the dressing room, Lily had learned not only fourth position but fifth position too, and not only one fourth position but two of them.

Lily had her problems, but Mrs. Howell spent more time with her than with anyone else, and Lily finally went from one fourth position to the next and then to fifth position, all in a row. She discovered that if she pictured a position in her mind before she assumed it with her body, she could get it right.

It was as if Miss Witt were reading her very thoughts!

"For this first class," she said, "it is permissible for you to *think*. You may think of the positions. And when you go home to practice this afternoon and evening, you may still think of them. But when you come back tomorrow, no more thinking! I want your *body* to have learned the positions. I want the positions to be part of your body. Not of your mind. A wheel need not think of how to turn before it turns. Your body must not think of how to dance before it dances. Am I understood? We shall see. Tomorrow we shall review the five positions of the feet. Then we shall learn the positions of the arms, which we should have learned today. You are a slow class. Dismissed!"

Once in the dressing room, Lily was sure she had forgotten *all* the positions. There was so much to learn, and it was only the first lesson. But Lily figured she had something that maybe no one else in the class had: a big sister who knew the positions so well that they must be part of her body. Saundra wouldn't have to teach her; that would be too much to ask. But she could certainly give Lily a little demonstration, a reminder, if Lily needed it. It must be so simple to Saundra, even though, right now, it seemed so complicated to Lily. But Lily knew she would get it. She would practice and practice. Afternoon and night. She couldn't wait to get home.

The dressing room was even more crowded than it had been before, and noisier and smellier. But Lily liked it now. She liked all the noise and the sweaty girls and even the sound of gum cracking in everyone's mouth. She brushed the back of her hand across her forehead and was delighted to find that she was sweaty too. And not just because it was summer. Dancing was hard work. It made you sweat. For a moment she had a picture in her mind of her father when he had returned from his jog around—well, not quite all the way around—the reservoir in Central Park. But sweating from jogging was one thing. And sweating from dancing was another. Dancing was beautiful. Jogging was just running. She wished her father would take up dancing instead of jogging. He had the tights, after all! Maybe she would take *him* to Capezio for some dancing shoes. But what about a leotard? The very thought made her chuckle.

Where were her clothes? She found the place where she'd left them, but someone had moved them, and her Capezio bag was no longer under them but on top of them.

Well, it didn't matter. Everything was there. Nothing had been stolen.

She found a place on a bench and sat down and pulled her arm through one of the straps of her leotard. But then she stopped. She felt like getting undressed. She felt like being naked—or almost, except for taking off her underpants—for what difference did it make? Obviously, dancers were always taking off one set of clothes and putting on another and then putting the first back on. No one noticed anyway what you had on, or didn't, and it was silly to hide when you got undressed.

But even more than being naked, she felt like keeping on her clothes. Her dance clothes.

So she took off only her ballet slippers and put them into her bag. She also put her sweatshirt and her socks into her bag. Then, because she couldn't take off her tights without first taking off her leotard, and that would be too much trouble, she simply slipped on her jeans over her tights. It might be hot going home that way. But it was a lot simpler. And she enjoyed the strong feeling in her legs from the tights.

She put on her sneakers and stood up. Her feet felt funny inside the sneakers, for the tights made them slip around. But she'd get used to it, she knew. She might even get used to wearing a leotard with jeans. It felt fine now. And it was rather ridiculous to wear a sweatshirt all summer anyway. A leotard was much cooler, even if it did hug your skin so tightly.

Lily stood up, took her bag in her hand by the strings, and turned to look for Saundra. She didn't see her, so she started to walk around the room, weaving among the many girls, being careful not to trip on all the outstretched legs of those sitting on the benches. But still no Saundra.

Maybe she would walk home. She felt so full of energy. But then Saundra would be looking for *her*, and when she didn't find her she would get all worried and probably angry. Lily remembered that she was Saundra's responsibility for today. But only for today—that should be enough of a deal to satisfy Saundra. And even though she felt she didn't need Saundra any longer, now that she'd had her first lesson, she knew she should wait for her. But how long would she be? Lily didn't want to wait. She wanted to go home and practice her positions.

Lily sat down on a bench to wait for Saundra. As she was waiting, trying to picture in her mind the five positions and imagining her feet assuming them, *thinking* of the positions, as Miss Witt had given the class permission to do this one time, someone said to her, "You're Saundra Leonard's sister, aren't you?"

Lily looked up and saw the girl who had made the dirty joke when Lily had been on her way to class: Meredith Meredith.

She was very beautiful, there was no denying that. As before, she had a soda in her hand and was chewing gum. But now she had changed from her sweaty leotard and was wearing an open pink frilly blouse and French jeans, just like Saundra's, except Meredith Meredith's were white. Her golden hair was tied up in a bun. Her eyes were blue and looked right into Lily's not only with haughtiness but also with impatience. The one thing Lily didn't think beautiful about Meredith Meredith was her mouth. Her lips were big, and they pouted. Saundra had Meredith Meredith beat in the mouth department. Otherwise . . . well, Lily had to admit it, Meredith Meredith was at least as beautiful as Saundra, and with that golden hair . . . It didn't matter. Meredith Meredith couldn't be as good a dancer as Saundra. Saundra was the best. She had to be. She *was*. Sometimes Lily wasn't at all sure that she even liked Saundra, who was skinny and beautiful and graceful and haughty. But she had to like her more than Meredith Meredith. Saundra was her sister. And Meredith Meredith looked even more haughty than Saundra, except for those droopy lips. Aside from which, any girl who had such a dirty mouth certainly didn't belong in the company of the American Ballet Center. A real dancer wouldn't speak that way— except Lily remembered what the tall woman at Capezio had said about how anyone could look like a dancer. Maybe someone who didn't *act* like a dancer when she wasn't dancing could be a dancer anyway. And Meredith Meredith certainly was beautiful. But she certainly had a disturbing look in her eye. When she asked Lily if she was Saundra Leonard's sister, and gazed straight into Lily's eyes, Lily found herself looking away. It was too hard to stare back at Meredith Meredith, it made her eyes sting.

Lily felt like saying, "What's it to you?" but instead she simply nodded.

"So I heard," said Meredith Meredith. She cracked her gum.

News travels fast around here, Lily thought.

"Tell me something," Meredith Meredith said. "Does your sister really think she's going to beat me out for a place in the company?"

Lily remembered her sister telling her that there

were other girls who were trying to beat her out for a place in the company, but Saundra hadn't mentioned anything about beating *them* out. It was interesting, now that she thought of it. How come Saundra *hadn't* said she was going to win? Saundra usually was confident about everything she did. Or at least she always seemed to be confident. But Lily knew she remembered correctly! Saundra had only said that she *wanted* the place in the company, not that she would get it.

However, Lily knew she shouldn't mention anything like that to Meredith Meredith. On the other hand, she couldn't lie to her. So she said, "No."

"She doesn't!" said Meredith Meredith. "Are you sure?"

"Yes."

"Just as I thought," said Meredith Meredith, though when she said it, Lily noticed, she took her eyes off Lily's and looked to the side. "She doesn't think she has a *chance* against me." She cracked her gum some more.

"I didn't say that," Lily said.

"You might as well have. If she doesn't *say* she thinks she's going to beat me out, then she doesn't *think* she's going to beat me out."

"But she didn't say anything about you," said Lily.

"It amounts to the same thing," said Meredith Meredith. "If she thought she was going to beat me out, she would have said she was going to beat me out."

"But she's never mentioned your name," said Lily.

"What!"

"She's never mentioned your name," Lily repeated.

Meredith Meredith repeated herself also. "What!" Now she was looking fiercely into Lily's eyes, and her face started to turn red. Her lips were even shaking a little, as if she were either about to cry or scream.

"Never," said Lily, enjoying the effect of telling the truth to Meredith Meredith and watching her get upset.

"Never mentioned my name!" She chewed her gum furiously now, but somehow she couldn't seem to make it crack.

"Never," said Lily again.

Meredith Meredith's lips started shaking so much, Lily thought they might start flapping around and making funny noises. But all of a sudden, Meredith Meredith took a deep breath, and then another, lifting her wide, bony shoulders almost to the top of her head. By the time her shoulders came back to join the rest of her body, she had regained her composure. Even her lips were almost motionless; just a small twitch in the bottom one made Lily realize that she was still upset.

"I don't believe you," said Meredith Meredith.

"It's true," said Lily.

"I still don't believe you. For your sister not to mention me is like oil not mentioning water."

"What?"

"They don't mix," said Meredith Meredith.

"Oh," said Lily.

"Like oil not mentioning water," repeated Meredith Meredith.

"I didn't know they could talk," Lily said.

"Very funny," said Meredith Meredith.

"Thank you," said Lily, who had meant it as a joke anyway. But Meredith Meredith was not laughing.

"About as funny as you *look*," said Meredith Meredith.

Lily didn't have an answer for that one.

"You're the funniest-looking thing I ever saw," said Meredith Meredith.

Still Lily had nothing to say.

"And I'll bet you can't dance either," said Meredith Meredith.

"I can't," said Lily. "But I'm going to learn."

"Save your calories," said Meredith Meredith. "You're too funny-looking to dance anyway."

"You don't have to be a dancer to look like a dancer," Lily said. "And you don't have to look like a dancer to be one. All you have to do is dance to be a dancer."

Now it was Meredith Meredith who had nothing to say. She stood there looking at Lily with hatred in her eyes. Then, just as her lips started to shake again, she said, "Tell your sister Saundra that I'm going to beat her out." Lily could see the gum sticking out from between Meredith Meredith's shaking lips.

"Sure," said Lily. "I'll tell her. But it's not true." Then she thought of something. Oh, this would really get to Meredith Meredith. "By the way—what's your real name?" she asked.

"Meredith Meredith," said Meredith Meredith proudly.

"Sure," said Lily. "And my name is Lily Lily."

"Go to hell," said Meredith Meredith, turning around and starting to walk away. "And tell your sister to go to hell too." And with that, she took a deep breath, lifted her shoulders up to the top of her head, and disappeared into the crowd of other girls.

As Lily watched her walk away, she saw Saundra.

Saundra was standing at the other side of the room, staring at Lily. She was staring at her with an even fiercer look in her eyes than Meredith Meredith had had. Lily had never seen her sister look quite like that.

"Hi, Saundra," she said, approaching her.

"Go to hell," said Saundra.

"What!" said Lily, thinking, *Not you too, Saundra, not you too*.

"Go to hell."

Lily could feel tears coming to her eyes. "What did I do wrong?" she said.

"As if you have to ask," said Saundra.

"But I don't know," said Lily, trying very hard not to cry.

"You can't be that stupid."

"Yes, I can," said Lily, feeling stupid and sad at the same time.

"You're a traitor," said Saundra.

"What do you mean?"

"I told you you were stupid. You don't even know what that word means."

"I know what it means," said Lily. "But I don't know what *you* mean."

"I'll tell you what I mean," said Saundra. "I mean this: You were standing over there talking to Meredith Meredith, and she's the worst enemy I have in the world. Even my other enemies wouldn't talk to her in front of me."

"But I didn't know you were there," said Lily.

"See!" said Saundra. "That makes you an even worse traitor. You thought you were talking to her behind my back."

"But *she* talked to *me*," said Lily.

"I saw you talking to her," answered Saundra. "Are you going to have the nerve to tell me you weren't talking to her, when I saw you with my own two eyes?"

"No," said Lily, still sad but also getting angry. Once again, she told the truth. "I was talking to her."

"I hate you," said Saundra. "I hate you as much as I hate her."

Lily started to cry. She looked at her sister through her tears and realized that her crying was not making Saundra feel bad for what she had said but was embarrassing her in front of all the other girls.

Saundra fidgeted with her canvas bag. Then she reached out and grabbed Lily's arm very hard and said, "Let's get out of here."

It was the last thing Saundra said to her on the whole trip home.

At dinner that night, everyone was very glad to hear that Lily had enjoyed her class. Everyone but Saundra, that is. All Saundra mentioned was their "deal."

"We have a deal," Saundra said.

"We do not," Lily said.

"What deal?" their father asked.

"We have a deal. A deal is a deal. And that's all I'm going to say." Saundra threw her napkin onto her plate and stalked off toward their room.

No one spoke for a moment.

Then Judge Leonard said, "She seems to be upset about something. What's this about a deal?"

"Nothing," said Lily.

"Good," said her mother. "Deal making has no place in a family."

"May I practice in the living room?" Lily asked.

"Practice what?" asked her father.

"My dance positions."

"Of course!" he said. "That's my girl—wants to

practice already. You'll be the best in your class if you keep this up."

"What's wrong with practicing in your bedroom?" asked her mother.

Lily didn't know what to say. She didn't want to tell them that she was afraid of Saundra, who seemed to think they really did have a deal and that Lily was never going back to dancing school.

Her father came to her rescue. "Must be this deal they have," he said. "Saundra gets to practice in the bedroom, and Lily has to find some other place."

"Just this once," said her mother. "The living room is for living, not for dancing."

"To a dancer, living and dancing are the same thing," said Lily.

"You're not a dancer yet," said her mother.

"True, true," said her father, reaching over to pat Lily's shoulder. "And it doesn't come easy. But my huggable bug will get there if she really works. Don't you worry about that."

"I'm not worried," said Lily. She started to rise from her chair. As she did so, she realized that her legs hurt, that they were very stiff.

Her mother said, "Oh, and one more thing. No more leotards at the table."

"It sure beats the sweatshirt," said her father.

"You may have a point," said her mother. "Lily, we'll discuss it another time."

Lily hardly heard her. Her legs were so stiff that she

could only hobble away. She couldn't imagine how she could possibly practice anything tonight.

Dancing, it turned out, was even harder work than she had thought, even when she was in the middle of dancing. It was hard work even when you weren't dancing.

·10·
A Conversation in a Dark Bedroom

"Can I talk to you, Saundra?"

"No."

"Please let me talk to you."

"No."

"I have to talk to you."

"No."

"Will you just listen if *I* talk?"

"No."

"Please."

"No."

"But I want to tell you—"

"Go to sleep, Lily."

"Saundra, please. Just for a few minutes."

"Go to sleep."

"I can't. I can't sleep."

"That's your tough luck."

"I won't be able to sleep until I can talk to you."

"No. Now shut up. I'm going to sleep. I have a very hard class tomorrow."

"You do? Tell me about it."

"There's nothing to tell."

"What's so hard about it?"

"Nothing in particular. It's just hard, that's all."

"It's always hard, I guess. Is it always hard, Saundra?"

"Yes, it's always hard."

"But it's worth it, isn't it? It always feels good after, doesn't it?"

"It feels terrible sometimes."

"What do you mean? Like you're stiff and your feet hurt?"

"That too, but—"

"I was stiff just today! I know exactly what you mean."

"It hurts more in your mind."

"What do you mean?"

"It hurts more to know that you were crappy."

"Crappy?"

"That you danced terribly today, that you danced terribly yesterday, and that you'll probably dance terribly tomorrow."

"Then why do you do it?"

"Because sometimes you think that tomorrow, tomorrow you'll dance beautifully."

"Maybe you will."

"Yes. Maybe I will. Now, go to sleep, Lily."

"But I have to talk to you."

"I have nothing to say to you. Not after what you did to me today."

"But what did I do?"

"I don't want to go into it again."

"But you never did go into it."

"And I'm not going into it now."

"Please. Just a short discussion."

"No."

"Okay. Can I ask you a question? About something else, I mean?"

"What?"

"How come you don't chew gum?"

"What kind of question is that?"

"I noticed that almost everyone else at dancing school—or at least all the older girls—they all chew gum. But you don't."

"I guess I don't."

"How come? Because it looks so vulgar?"

"Where did you learn that word?"

"From Mom. So is that why you don't chew gum? Because it's vulgar?"

"No."

"Because you don't like the taste, then?"

"I like the taste all right."

"Then why don't you chew gum?"

"I don't like what it does to the shape of my jaw."

"You have a great jaw. I wish *I* had a jaw like yours. Your jaw is so haughty."

"Where did you learn that word? As if I have to ask."

"Mom again."

"So I have a haughty jaw, huh?"

"You know what I mean. But what does chewing gum have to do with it?"

"It changes the shape of your jaw."

"It does?"

"Certainly. Think of how many times you chew a single piece of gum. Then think of how many pieces of gum you would chew in a day. Then think of how many days you chew gum in a year. Then multiply."

"I can't. Not in my head, anyway."

"I didn't mean for you to do the arithmetic. I just meant for you to think of what so much chewing would do to your jaw."

"Oh. Then how come all the other girls chew gum all the time?"

"They're nervous."

"Are you nervous?"

"Sometimes."

"So how come you don't chew gum?"

"I told you. I don't like what it does to the shape of my jaw."

"But what does it do exactly?"

"It lowers it."

"It lowers what?"

"My jaw, stupid."

"You mean, it makes it less haughty."

"If you want to put it that way."

"Why do you want a haughty jaw anyway?"

"Why do *you* want one?"

"Me?"

"Yes. You said you want a jaw like mine. Just a minute ago."

"Gee. I guess you're right."

"But then, Lily, you're not a person who remembers anything she says."

"I do too."

"What about our *deal*, Lily?"

"We don't have a deal."

"Oh yes we do. You were supposed to tell Mom and Dad that you hated dancing school and you never wanted to go back again."

"But I didn't hate it."

"But you *thought* you would."

"I know it."

"And you were supposed to tell them that you did."

"No I wasn't. And I didn't."

"I know you didn't."

"I mean I didn't hate it."

"And I mean you didn't tell them."

"I told them the truth."

"Then you lied to me."

"No I didn't."

"Yes you did. We had a deal."

"I never said we did."

"We had a deal, Lily. That's all there is to it. We had a deal, and you're breaking our deal. It's the last deal we're ever going to have."

"But we *didn't*. *You* said we had a deal. *I* never said we did."

"Go to sleep. I don't want to talk about it anymore. It's making me angry, and if I get angry, I won't be able to sleep. And I don't even want to think about how you were talking to Meredith Meredith. Go to sleep. Leave me alone."

"I can't go to sleep."

"That's your problem."

"But I wasn't talking to Meredith Meredith. I mean—I was talking to her, but it wasn't what you think. Saundra? Are you listening? Saundra. Talk to me. I need to talk to you. Saundra? Saundra?"

·11·
Ugly Feet Are Beautiful

Soon Lily could hear Saundra breathing deeply. She knew her sister was asleep and that she couldn't talk to her any longer. But she still had so much to say. All the words were running through her mind. She could speak them and hear them inside her head. And they kept her awake.

They were words about their deal that wasn't a deal. They were words about Meredith Meredith and what Lily had really said to her. They were words that were questions about dancing. They were words that said, "Why don't you like me, Saundra? I'm your sister. Why don't you like me?" They were words from Lily to comfort Saundra, words to tell her that she was a terrific dancer and she would get the place in the company of the American Ballet Center and Lily would come to see her dance in the theater and would shower applause on her until her hands hurt as much as Saundra's feet hurt.

So many words. And all so silent. Saundra didn't hear one of them. They all remained shut up in Lily's head. Pounding and pleading. They kept her awake for hours. She felt as if she had electricity on her skin. And a radio inside her head.

She tried to make herself go to sleep by thinking of dancing. She pictured herself in class, assuming first position, second position, all the positions, getting better with each one while the rest of the class went on struggling to keep their balance and not look foolish. Then she saw Miss Witt get up from her stool and come over to her and say, "You're really very good, Curly. What else can you do?" And at that, Lily let go of the *barre*, pranced across the room, leaped into the air, leaped again, fluttered through space, turned, twirled, turned, twirled, ran on her toes from one side of the room to the other, flew like a bird through the air. But as she saw herself do this in her mind, she saw that she looked more like Saundra than herself. And she realized that she, Lily, couldn't do any of this, and that Saundra—Saundra, who was fast asleep just across the room—could do it all. For Saundra it wasn't a dream. Saundra was a dancer.

Lily wondered what it felt like to dance. She knew she herself was just at the beginning. She had had only one lesson, after all. One lesson! That was nothing.

But Saundra had been dancing almost every day for almost six years. Day after day, Saundra had packed her leotard and tights and shoes in her bag and had gone off to class. Before today, Lily hadn't had even an idea of what a dancing class looked like. The big room. The *barre* on one side. The mirror on the other. The piano player, who hadn't even been given a chance to play and spent the whole class slurping his coffee and reading his magazine.

Almost every day of her life for the past six years, Saundra had been going off to such a room. It amazed Lily to think that one day, almost six years ago, Saundra had been the same age as Lily was now and had gone off to her very first class, just as Lily had today. Lily wondered if Saundra, too, had hated the idea of going to class before she ever went to one, and then, after her first class, had decided that she loved to dance. Lily wondered if Saundra's legs had gotten stiff after her first class.

It was impossible to sleep. There was so much to think about.

Lily threw off her thin summer blanket and sat up in bed. In the light from the streetlamp she could see clearly her feet sticking out from the bottom of her nightgown. Across the room Saundra was visible too, sleeping on her back, not covered by a blanket or even a sheet, her body stretched out, one leg straight, the other curled up in an L shape so that one foot rested on the other knee. It was as if Saundra, even sleeping, was dancing too. Lily could not deny it. Saundra was very beautiful and very graceful.

But what about her feet? Was it true, as her father had told her, that all dancers had ugly feet? And what had Saundra meant when she told Lily in the dressing room, "Worry about your feet," and had pointed to the girl next to her, the girl with the bloody feet? What about Saundra? What about Saundra's feet?

Lily slowly got up from the bed and walked as quietly as possible over to Saundra. She knelt down by Saundra's feet and looked at them, first at the one toward the bottom of the bed, then at the one that was resting on the other knee.

They looked perfectly fine to her. But the light in the room—the light from the streetlamp, for there was no moon—wasn't strong enough for close inspection of anything.

So Lily rose, being careful not to lean on Saundra's bed or to make any noise, and went to her closet. There—packed in with her sleeping bag and ice skates and the old bugle her father had given her but on which she'd never learned to play a single note or even to blow a single sound—was her flashlight. Because Saundra had never wanted a nightlight on in the room, Lily used to keep the flashlight next to her bed, when she was younger and frightened of the dark. But now she hardly ever used it.

Lily tested the flashlight in the closet. It gave off a dim light. She went back to Saundra's bed and shined the flashlight on her sister's foot that was closest to the end of the bed.

Lily stared at each toe. Then she shook her head. It was hard to believe.

She shined the flashlight on the other foot. The toes were the same. But on this foot she could also see the bottom. She shook her head again and leaned closer to get an even better look.

It was unbelievable.

Almost every one of Saundra's toenails was black. One of the toenails was missing completely. Another one was separated from the toe and just kind of hanging there, ready to fall off.

The bottoms of her feet were all scaly, covered with thick skin that looked hard and shiny and rough.

Lily was fascinated. She couldn't take her eyes off Saundra's feet. They were kind of sickening. But at the same time, they were kind of beautiful. There was no question that her feet were ugly. But they were also beautiful.

"What are you looking at?"

Saundra's voice, in the dimly lit room, breaking into her concentration on Saundra's feet, almost made Lily jump. As it was, she dropped the flashlight, which landed on Saundra's shin.

"Ouch!" said Saundra.

"Sorry," said Lily meekly.

"What are you *doing?* "

"I lost something," Lily said.

"What?"

"I said, I lost something."

"No. I mean, *what* did you lose?"

Lily thought for a moment. It was no good to lie. "Nothing," she said.

"Did you or didn't you lose something?"

"No."

"You didn't?"

"No."

"Then what were you doing?"

"Looking at your feet."

"You were looking at my feet!" Saundra sounded really upset.

"Yes."

"That's an invasion of my privacy."

"I'm sorry," Lily apologized.

"Why were you looking at my feet?"

"I wanted to see them."

"In the middle of the night?"

"Well," said Lily, "you always keep them covered up in the daytime."

"I know I do. Did it ever occur to you why?"

"No."

"Well, now that you've seen them, Lily—*now* do you know why I keep them covered up?"

"I guess," said Lily.

"Why?" Saundra asked again.

Lily said nothing.

"I'll tell you why," said Saundra. "I'll *show* you

why." She picked up the flashlight and shined it on her right foot. "Look at it," she ordered. "Look at it."

Lily looked.

"Take a good look," said Saundra.

Lily took a long look.

"That's why I hide them. Because they look like that."

Lily realized that Saundra had begun to cry.

"What's the matter?" she asked.

"Oh, nothing!" said Saundra, sniffling, obviously trying to make her tears go away by speaking gruffly.

"But they're beautiful," said Lily.

Saundra actually broke into laughter, even though she was still crying. "Oh, Lily," she said. "They're ugly. They're not beautiful. They're ugly. But that's not what's the matter. All dancers' feet are ugly. Mine are too. There's nothing you can do about it."

"So why are you crying?" asked Lily.

"I'm crying because I don't know if it's worth it."

"What do you mean?"

"I don't care if I have the ugliest feet in the world," said Saundra, "if I can be a great dancer. But what if I can't?"

"You already are."

Saundra stopped crying. She shook her head. "What if I can't?" she asked again. "Then what? Then it's not worth it. It's not worth having feet like this. It's not worth hurting your body. It's not worth spending almost every waking minute practicing and studying and not thinking about anything else or doing anything else. It's not worth thinking that you're committing a sin against your body every time you eat an ice cream cone. It's not worth it."

"I think it is," said Lily.

"How can you say that? What do you know about it? You've taken only one class, Lily. What can you possibly know about it?"

"I just think it's worth it," Lily said.

"But why?"

"It would be worth it to me if I could dance like you."

"You really think so?"

"Yes. And I think your feet are beautiful. I think you have beautiful feet."

"You must be blind."

"To me they're beautiful."

"Go to bed, Lily. It's the middle of the night. And you don't know what you're talking about. Go to bed."

Lily got up off her knees and walked back to her bed. As she covered herself with her thin blanket, she realized she hadn't seen or heard Saundra cry in years. It made her feel funny. It made her feel that her sister was even more beautiful than before, but less haughty. She wished she could help Saundra so she wouldn't cry anymore. Or else, so she would cry whenever she wanted to. Maybe Saundra was afraid. Maybe Saundra, deep down inside, was scared of dancing. Maybe she was scared of not dancing well enough to beat out

Meredith Meredith for the place in the company. Maybe she was scared of being just an ordinary person who would never get up on a stage and have people applaud her until their hands ached and her own ears tingled with excitement.

To Lily, Saundra was not an ordinary person. But maybe to herself she was. It was hard to believe. But maybe she was, and all her haughty looks and her dancer's proud walk just hid what she felt inside: that she was an ordinary person.

"Good night, Saundra," Lily whispered across the room.

There was no answer.

"You're a special person," Lily said softly.

She listened hard for a response. All she finally heard, before she drifted off to sleep, was the sound of quiet crying.

·12·
Peaking

Over the next several weeks, Lily went every day but Sunday to class at the American Ballet Center. She took the bus with Saundra, and walked the block from Central Park West to Broadway with Saundra, and each day she hoped that Saundra would talk to her, take her into her confidence about Saundra's feelings, her fears and her hopes. But as time went on, Saundra stopped saying even little things like "Here's where we get off" or "Ring the bell" or "Hurry up." It wasn't long, in fact, before Saundra stopped talking to Lily altogether. And Lily was afraid to ask her sister questions.

Saundra had changed in other ways too. She no longer seemed to sit so straight and haughtily. Not that she slumped—but she seemed tired, and nervous, so that her body was both rigid and almost a little shaky at the same time. Nor did she stare out the window for the whole trip. Instead, her eyes darted around the bus, looking from face to face, never stopping for more than a moment on any one person. And none of the people really looked back at Saundra, let alone stared at her, the way they had when Lily first rode to school with her. Saundra was just like anyone else—merely another passenger on the bus, going to wherever she was going, not really noticed by the other passengers.

Lily thought she knew what was happening to Saundra. Saundra was working too hard to prepare for her audition for the place in the second company of the American Ballet Center.

Saundra had not said anything about it. But Lily had overheard their parents talking about how Saundra might be getting tired and how she was losing weight and how she was training so much that she might "peak." Lily didn't know what it meant if you "peaked," so one day she asked her father when he came home from the park in his jogging suit if you could peak if you were a jogger, and he said that you could, if you were a real runner and you were training for a race. It meant that you got to be too good too fast, and not in a real race but in practice. In other words, Lily decided, maybe Saundra had practiced *too* much and was not going to dance as well during her actual audition as she had when she was practicing in the weeks before.

During one bus ride to school, Lily worked up her courage and said to Saundra, "Be careful not to peak."

Saundra continued to look around at all the faces on the bus for a long time but then let her eyes rest on Lily's. There was an angry look on Saundra's face. She said nothing. But she continued to stare at Lily, as if to say, "How dare you speak to me." Lily looked away.

And then, once they had gotten off the bus and walked halfway down the block toward the school, Saundra said, "Don't worry. I'm not peaking."

In the past, Lily might have made a joke and pretended that Saundra had meant "peeking" instead of "peaking." She might have said, "Peeking at what? Are my underpants showing?" But now she just nodded. Saundra was in no mood for jokes. Not that she ever really had been, but Lily had sometimes tried to make her laugh, or at least smile that strange smile of hers. But now she couldn't imagine Saundra laughing or even smiling at anything. Saundra had become so serious a person that she seemed almost sad, sad all the time.

Lily waited for Saundra to say some more about peaking, or not peaking, but she didn't and merely walked on. Her strides were not as long as they used to be, so Lily didn't have as much trouble keeping up. Sometimes Lily even had to slow down her own walk so that Saundra could keep up. The closer they got to the school, the more slowly Saundra walked. It was as if she didn't really want to go.

Lily, on the other hand, loved school. She couldn't wait to get there every day.

The dressing room no longer frightened her. She always managed to find a place on one of the benches. And although she had started to wear a leotard all the time with her jeans—it really *was* too hot in the summer for a sweatshirt, she couldn't imagine why she hadn't *roasted* every other summer—she didn't wear the same one to dance in. She'd gone back to Capezio twice with her father and had picked out more leotards and tights, all in different colors. The tall woman had remembered her each time. She said she was happy that Lily had learned to love dancing school.

She was also learning to dance and to love to dance.

She mastered the positions, all but the fourth, which Miss Witt said was too advanced for the class. From the positions of the feet, the class moved to positions of the arms, which they matched up with the positions of the feet. They used mostly the Cecchetti Method, though Miss Witt also showed them how the arm positions were different in the French School and the Russian School. Lily couldn't keep it all straight at first, but she practiced at home and pretty soon had learned to keep up with the class. She wasn't the best, but she wasn't the worst.

The best was one of the two boys.

Not the fat one, whose name was Yuri and whose mother had been a famous Russian ballerina; Yuri was having a little less trouble in school, but he still fell down once or twice, and Miss Witt and Mrs. Howell now let him get up by himself, which he always managed finally to do, laughing as he did so.

Hector was the name of the boy who was the best dancer in the class. He was Puerto Rican and always wore a green leotard. Although he was smaller than Lily and looked much younger, he was a year older. Lily once overheard Miss Witt tell him that he shouldn't worry about his size: Nureyev and Baryshnikov, she said, were small men also, and the important thing was strength, and of course grace, not size.

Hector was Miss Witt's pet. Lily sometimes had the feeling that Miss Witt didn't think anyone else in the whole class could really be a dancer. But this didn't mean that Miss Witt was sweet to Hector. In fact, she criticized him all the time. At first, this confused Lily. She thought Miss Witt was being terribly mean to Hector by continually correcting his dancing in front of the whole class.

Then one day Miss Witt corrected *her*. But rather than feeling embarrassed at being corrected, Lily had a sense of being special. She had been doing the exercises—*grands pliés* in all the positions but the fourth, which meant that you bent your knees until your thighs were horizontal—better than most of the other children in the class. And yet it was she whom Miss

Witt corrected. "Heels up too soon, Curly!" Miss Witt said, as Lily descended into the *grand plié* in the fifth position. "Heels on the floor until your knees are bent halfway." Lily tried it. As she did so, Miss Witt said, "Back straight . . . knees bending . . . heels down . . . knees bending . . . heels *up* . . . keep going . . . slowly slowly . . . very well . . . now rise . . . slowly . . . slowly . . . heels down . . . press up . . . fine, fine. Practice that more, Curly."

It was then that Lily realized it was a privilege to be corrected. Miss Witt always corrected Hector. And there were a few girls whom she also corrected every now and then. They were, Lily realized, some of the best dancers in the class. Now Miss Witt had corrected her. It must mean there was some hope for her after all. Maybe she really might be good enough to be a dancer.

No, she wasn't the best. But she certainly wasn't the worst, as she had feared she might be before she had gone even to the first class.

She was learning. That was the important thing. She was learning how to dance. Every day, every class, taught her a little more. Every day, every class, and every practice session at home, even if she just stretched, as Saundra always did at home—every day she grew a little stronger at the same time that she also grew a little looser in her body, in her muscles and her joints. You didn't have to be tight in order to be strong. You should be strong and flexible at the same time. You should be able to control your body and make it do whatever you want it to do, which means that it must be both strong and loose.

Lily was learning. But she would have been able to learn so much faster if only she had been able to talk to Saundra. Lily now knew it for a fact that Saundra was one of the best dancers at the school. The other students talked about Saundra all the time, especially now that the audition was getting closer. Some of them tried to talk to *her* about Saundra. But Lily pretended to them that she respected Saundra's privacy too much to discuss her with other people. The fact of the matter was that she didn't really know very much about Saundra. All she knew was that lately Saundra was getting more tired and more nervous. And Lily would never dare breathe a word about that. She didn't want to give Saundra's competitors for the position in the company any hint that Saundra might be peaking or that she was scared of not being good enough to win the position.

The Slap

Ever since Saundra had accused Lily of being a traitor for having spoken to Meredith Meredith in the dressing room after Lily's first class at the American Ballet Center, Lily had gone out of her way to avoid Meredith Meredith.

It wasn't so difficult. Often, Meredith Meredith wasn't in the dressing room when Lily was there. And when Meredith Meredith was there, she was usually surrounded by a bunch of girls, all of them chewing gum and drinking diet soda out of cans, just like Meredith Meredith, and all of them trying to get in the next word with Meredith Meredith. It was clear that these girls were just sucking up to her, as if they could be as good dancers as she was if she would speak to them, as if knowing Meredith Meredith and being seen talking to her would make other people think more highly of them. As far as Lily was concerned, these girls were what her father called "lickers": they went around with their tongues hanging out, they licked whatever looked good, but they never got more than a tiny taste of anything and never knew whether what they did lick tasted good or bad. Such people had "blind tongues," her father said, and, he would add, "they don't see so well either." He also called them "phonies." And "psycho pants," whatever that meant—it sounded to Lily as if it had something to do with wearing crazy trousers, maybe blue jeans that had lost their minds, except that didn't make any sense.

The important thing to Lily was that she didn't have to talk to Meredith Meredith, whom she didn't like in the first place and who could get her in a lot of trouble with her sister if Saundra were to see them talking together.

Several times, though, Meredith Meredith happened to walk right by Lily, either when Lily was busy or preoccupied and didn't see her coming or when the crowd in the dressing room made it impossible for Lily to move away from the approaching Meredith Meredith.

But on these occasions Meredith Meredith either ignored Lily completely—maybe she didn't even see her—or else glared at her or, only once, spoke to her.

That time she said to Lily, as she walked by her: "Tell your sister she doesn't have a chance."

Of course Lily had no intention of telling Saundra *anything* Meredith Meredith might have said to her, let alone repeating something as mean as that. What Lily had wanted to do was say right back to Meredith Meredith, "She does too," or, "Neither do you," or, "Shut up," or even, "Go to hell," which is what Meredith Meredith had said to her on Lily's first day at dancing school. But none of these sounded very convincing. Aside from which, Lily just didn't want to take the chance of being seen by Saundra saying *anything* to Meredith Meredith.

And so Lily really didn't know what to do when one day, after class, Meredith Meredith appeared at her side as she was sitting on a bench changing into her street clothes, tapped Lily on the shoulder, and said, "What happened to your sister?"

Lily wanted to ignore Meredith Meredith, but she was frightened. Had something really happened to Saundra? She had to know. "What?" she asked.

"I said, what happened to your sister?" Meredith Meredith cracked her gum and looked down at Lily, waiting for a reply.

"I heard you the first time," said Lily.

"So?" said Meredith Meredith, putting her hand on her hip and tilting the hip upward at the same time. She certainly was thin and graceful, Lily thought, and she hated herself for thinking nice things about her sister's enemy. Meredith Meredith was wearing a sweaty leotard and had a towel wrapped around her neck, where some wet strands of hair hung down. Lily tried to feel disgust at this sweating person standing next to her, but it was impossible: sweating was beautiful. Meredith Meredith was beautiful—there was no denying it. Even her mouth didn't look so bad today. Her lips were still enormous, but they seemed to fit her face better, maybe because she was still in her dance clothes, which made her whole body, and especially her wide, thin shoulders, seem bigger. Lily looked at her and could think no ugly thoughts to have about her—except that she was not a very nice person, which didn't seem to matter when it came to being a dancer.

"You certainly have a slow mind," said Meredith Meredith, who stood there rocking her hip, her hand still on it, as she stared at Lily.

"Oh, I'm sorry," said Lily. "I was just thinking." She realized that she'd forgotten what she was going to say. She'd even forgotten what they were talking about—until she remembered that something might have happened to Saundra. "What happened to my sister?" she blurted out.

"Oh, God, are you stupid!" said Meredith Meredith. "That's what I was asking *you*. Your face was so blank—I should have known. What *were* you thinking about?"

"You," said Lily.

"Me?"

"Yes. That's why I had a blank look."

"Oh, shut up," said Meredith Meredith.

"Likewise," said Lily, thinking that her mother hated the expression "shut up" but couldn't possibly have any objection to a nice word like "likewise."

Lily rose from the bench, slipped her Capezio bag over her wrist, and turned to go. She would find Saundra herself. If anything had really happened to her, the other girls would have been talking about it among themselves. Saundra was still a big star to all the other girls. She was still the best dancer, Lily was certain of it.

"Where do you think you're going?" asked Meredith Meredith.

"To find my sister," Lily answered.

"Well, give her a message for me. Tell her she doesn't have a chance."

"I will *not!* " said Lily.

"Then don't," said Meredith Meredith. "Let her make a fool of herself. Anybody with eyes can see that she's falling apart. She *doesn't* have a chance. She doesn't have a *chance.* "

"She'll beat *you* out," said Lily, feeling angry.

"Listen to me, you funny-looking thing. Even *you* could beat her out, the way she's dancing these days. Even you, if you can believe it! And I hear you're *terrible.* "

Lily took a deep breath to control her anger and her

desire to hit this girl or to cry, and said, "I'm just a beginner. What do you expect?"

"Of you, nothing. Of your sister, at least a little competition. She's making it too *easy* for me. I hardly have to practice. I might even be getting fat." Meredith Meredith took her thumb and first finger and pinched herself at her hip. She could hardly find even some skin to hold on to. She laughed. "Well, not too fat—not as fat as you." She put her hand on Lily's hip and squeezed her flesh in all her fingers. Lily flinched. It hurt. But she said nothing.

Meredith Meredith squeezed harder. Still Lily said nothing, but it hurt enough to bring tears to her eyes.

Don't touch the merchandise, she screamed in her mind. Don't touch the merchandise!

Meredith Meredith put her other hand on Lily's other hip. She now squeezed with both hands. Lily thought she might jump right off her feet, it hurt so much.

At the moment she couldn't stand it any longer, she raised her arm, drew it back, and slapped Meredith Meredith hard across the cheek.

Meredith Meredith let go of Lily and raised her shoulders and brought both her hands up to her face, which was red on both sides but mostly on the side where Lily could still see the outline of her own fingers peeking out from beneath Meredith Meredith's hands.

Lily realized with a shock that the whole dressing room was quiet, that the usual buzzing of voices and cracking of gum and thumping of toe shoes were suddenly turned off. People had heard the slap. They were all watching, silently, to see what would happen next.

Meredith Meredith stood there holding her face. She was like a statue. Nothing moved. She just stared at Lily as if she couldn't believe what Lily had done to her.

Without thinking, Lily sensed that this was her chance to escape—before Meredith Meredith did start to move, expecially if her next move was to take a swing at Lily. Meredith Meredith had never looked more enormous. Her shoulders seemed to take up half the room, as they bunched around her head.

Lily turned, scared that Meredith Meredith might hit her in the back—and there, staring at her, was Saundra, just a few feet away.

Oh, no, thought Lily. Oh, no.

She was so afraid that Saundra hadn't seen anything except that she and Meredith Meredith were together. It was almost worth turning around again and going toward Meredith Meredith and away from Saundra, if Saundra was going to hate her again.

But there was no turning back.

She had taken only a step or two before Saundra held out her hand, and Lily nearly tripped in her rush to grab it.

·14·
Friends

They were at home in their bedroom.

"Tell me, Saundra. Tell me. Tell me," Lily was pleading.

Saundra sat on her bed. Lily sat next to her. Saundra had her elbows on her knees and held her chin in her hands. She was bent over, staring into the room. Lily wanted to tell her to sit up straight. Saundra didn't look like a dancer, sitting like that. Even her feet were flat on the floor, her toes not pointed, her arches not poised. Her whole body sagged. She was too thin. She seemed to have no energy.

So far nothing had worked. Lily couldn't get Saundra to say anything, to tell her what was the matter.

It's true that Saundra had continued to hold Lily's hand on the walk to the bus and then for the whole ride home. But she still hadn't said a word to her. Nothing.

"Please," said Lily. "Say something. Tell me what's the matter."

Saundra just shook her head, as it lay in her hands.

Lily got up from the bed.

"Shall I dance for you?" she asked.

Saundra raised her eyes.

"Want to see what I've learned?" Lily said.

Saundra nodded. Just a little. But she nodded. Lily couldn't believe it.

"Really?" Lily asked.

Saundra nodded again.

"Wait a minute," said Lily.

She found one of her Capezio bags. It was lying in a heap against the wall near her bed, along with her other Capezio bags. As Lily fished in it for a pair of dancing shoes, she realized that her own collection of bags was beginning to make just as much of a mess as Saundra's. But now it seemed natural to her. Now she understood. When you are a dancer, you are tired when you get home. You don't want to put everything away all neatly in its place. You want to lie down and rest your weary body. You also want to dance, or at least to stretch your tired bones. The last thing you want to do is clean up. It doesn't even seem right to clean up. Dancing is the cleanest thing in the world. Your dancing things belong together, in their bags, in your room, dreaming, the way you dream, of the next dance.

Lily took off her jeans. She didn't want to take off her leotard and put on tights, so she just put her dancing slippers on her bare feet. Then she stood in the middle of the room, facing Saundra.

"What do you want me to do?" she asked.

"Anything," said Saundra. It was the first word she had spoken.

"Here's a *tendu*, " said Lily, and she did a *battement tendu* from the first position to the second, one foot planted on the floor, the other flexed as it slid, both knees straight. When she had returned the foot and was back in first position, she did a little *fouetté*, raising her foot and whipping it in front of the other leg and then behind it. She had just learned this. That was why her leg moved in a jerky motion.

"Try it again," said Saundra.

Lily did, and this time her movement was smoother.

"Better," said Saundra.

Lily smiled. "A *fondu?*" she asked.

Saundra nodded. "Hold on to the dresser," she said.

"Of course," said Lily, wondering if Saundra thought she could do it without holding on. Lily knew she wasn't ready for that.

She put one hand on her dresser and bent one leg

out in front of her and sank down on the other leg until she was halfway to the floor. She held the position, trying to keep her body as still as possible.

"Now let go," said Saundra.

"What?" said Lily.

"You heard me," Saundra said.

"Gee," said Lily, wondering if she could do it.

"Try it," said Saundra.

Lily let go, balancing on the foot of her bent leg. For a few moments she felt she could hold the position, but all of a sudden her leg started to shake, and she began to lose her balance. Just as she was about to reach out to grab the dresser, Saundra moved from the bed and put both her hands on Lily's hips. They were still sore from where Meredith Meredith had pinched them, but Saundra's grasp, which was strong and gentle at the same time, felt good. It was as if Saundra's hands were part of Lily's own body.

"Down," said Saundra.

"What?"

"Go down."

"More?"

"All the way."

"Gee."

"As far as you can," said Saundra, pressing her hands into Lily's hips.

Lily started to sink farther on her leg, still keeping the raised leg bent in front of her, even with the floor.

As Lily sank, Saundra dipped toward her, bending at the waist.

Lily realized that she was almost sitting on her own ankle. She was so far down. A muscle in her thigh twitched. The rest of her body was still. She was balanced and poised, so close to the floor but feeling as if at any moment she might spring up and fly around the room. It was a beautiful sensation.

"Now, come back up," said Saundra. "But slowly. Slowly, Lily. Like a fondue. You're melting. Melting. Melting up. Little bubbles. Not popping. Just swelling. Melting. That's good. That's good. There."

Once again, Lily was locked upright into place on her one leg, the other still out in front of her.

Saundra let go. Lily stood there and then put her arms in fifth position, up over her head, the fingertips almost touching.

"Beautiful," said Saundra.

Lily felt her mouth smile an enormous smile, just as she lost her balance. She fell into Saundra's arms and felt their strength around her.

Lily laughed. She looked up into Saundra's face and watched her sister start to laugh too.

Lily pushed against Saundra, pushed until she had moved both of them against Saundra's bed, onto which they fell, laughing.

"Just like when you were little," said Saundra.

"What do you mean?"

"You used to do that to me when you were little. You used to push against my legs. And I used to pretend I couldn't stop you. I used to fall backward onto the bed, and then you would crawl into my lap."

"Really?" said Lily.

"Don't you remember?" asked Saundra.

"Nope," said Lily.

"I do," said Saundra.

"Are you sure?" asked Lily, who thought she remembered everything.

"Of course I'm sure," answered Saundra. "You're the only sister I have. How could I forget?"

"How could *I* forget?" asked Lily.

"You were only a baby," said Saundra.

"But I'm not a baby anymore."

"Nope," said Saundra.

"So can we be friends?" asked Lily.

Saundra looked into Lily's face. She stared into her eyes. Then she gave one of her strange little smiles. The corners of her mouth turned up just slightly. Lily was glad to see it. But she told herself that someday she would have to teach Saundra how to really smile.

"We are now," said Saundra.

"What do you mean?"

"I'm sorry, Lily."

"For what?"

"That's what I couldn't say before. I'm sorry. I really am."

"For *what?*"

"For Meredith Meredith."

"You're sorry for *her!*" Lily couldn't believe her ears.

"Not for *her*," said Saundra. "For what she did to *you*."

"Well . . ." said Lily, starting to tell Saundra that Meredith Meredith hadn't really hurt her.

Saundra interrupted. "And I'm sorry for not stopping her."

"Did you see her?"

"Yes," said Saundra.

"Gee, so how come you didn't stop her?"

"I was afraid."

"What about me?" asked Lily.

"Were you afraid?"

Lily thought for a moment. "I guess not," she said. "But—"

"I know," interrupted Saundra. "I'm her age. I'm just as big as she is. And I could probably knock her head off, the skinny—"

"Don't swear," said Lily. "Besides—"

"I know. I've gotten even thinner than she is."

"How did you know what I was going to say?"

"You were looking at my ribcage."

"It *does* stick out."

"So what!"

"Don't get angry, Saundra."

"I'm sorry."

"That's okay. But you didn't tell me how come you're afraid of her."

"I don't know," said Saundra. "I can't explain it. It's just that I'm afraid. Every time I see her I almost begin to shake."

"It must be the audition."

"Don't be silly," said Saundra sharply. "I'm a better dancer than she is."

"She asked me what was the matter with you."

"What?"

"Meredith Meredith asked me what was the matter with you."

"She has some nerve!"

"Well . . ." Lily began. Then she stopped, not sure she should go on.

"What?"

"Nothing."

"Tell me what you were going to say," Saundra demanded.

"It's nothing."

"Lily . . ." Saundra looked at her with glaring eyes.

"Well," Lily began, "do you remember how I told you not to peak?"

Saundra nodded.

"Maybe you are peaking," Lily went on. "You seem so tired all the time. And you're getting so skinny. And even though you're tired, I know you don't sleep very well, because I can hear you tossing and turning in the middle of the night. And you seem . . ." Lily stopped.

"What? What do I seem?"

"Sad," said Lily.

"You know something, Lily?" asked Saundra, looking at her with softer eyes now.

"What?"

"I *feel* sad."

"You do?"

"I don't know how to explain it. I feel sad all the time." Lily reached out and put her hand on Saundra's knee. "And scared too. Sad and scared."

"Of what?"

"I don't know. Of nothing in particular. Of everything."

"Or maybe just of Meredith Meredith, as you said."

She waited for Saundra to say something, but Saundra just sat there looking at her, with a vacant expression on her face.

"So *are* you?" Lily finally asked.

"Am I what?"

"Scared of Meredith Meredith?"

"I said I was."

"But are you scared of her beating you out for the place in the company?"

"No. I said I'm a better dancer than she is."

"So why are you scared of her?"

"I don't know," said Saundra.

"I think you're scared of her beating you out for a place in the company," said Lily.

"Bullshit!" said Saundra.

"Swearing only makes me think it more."

"What do you know about it? How do you know I'm scared of her beating me out?"

"Because there's no other reason to be scared of her."

"There isn't?"

"Nope," said Lily. She raised her hand as if to hit someone. "I gave her a good one, and—"

"You sure did."

"I gave her a good one, and she didn't know what hit her."

"*You* hit her. My little sister."

"I sure did. Know why?"

"Why?"

"Because she hurt me. But even more because she said bad things about you."

"What bad things?"

"That she was going to beat you out for the company."

"Oh, she says that to everyone."

"Well, I don't like it when she says it to me. Because I know it's a lie. I know—"

"Lily," Saundra said, breaking in. "I'm afraid—that maybe she will beat me out. I *am*."

Lily knew Saundra was finally telling the truth. She

took her sister's hand in her own and squeezed it, wondering at the same time how she could possibly help Saundra to feel better and look better and dance better and get into the company.

·15·
Ask Lily

Just before going to bed, they went to kiss their parents good night. Judge and Mr. Leonard were sitting in the "room of many names." When it was used for reading, it was called the library; when it was used for watching television, it was called the TV room; when it was used for overnight visitors, it was called the guest bedroom; when it was used for naps, it was called the den; and when it wasn't being used for anything, it was called the room of many names or, for short, the spare room.

Tonight it needed two names. Their father was reading a book. Their mother was watching a baseball game on TV.

"Come on, Red Sox!" their mother was saying as Lily and Saundra entered.

"Why are you rooting for the Red Sox?" asked Lily.

She knew that the Boston Red Sox and the New York Yankees were arch rivals. Their mother was a New Yorker. So she should be rooting for the home team.

"Because they're at bat," Judge Leonard said. "I love to see the players get base hits. So I root for the team that's at bat. That way, I get to root for both teams."

Their father looked up from his book and toward his wife. He shook his head and smiled at her. "So much for the defense," he said, and Lily knew he was making a little joke about baseball and lawyering. He was a defense lawyer. Sometimes judges didn't seem to root for defense lawyers.

"Don't you care who wins?" Lily asked her mother.

"Not particularly," she answered. "It's only a game. I like the game, not the contest."

"Don't forget," said their father. "Your mother doesn't believe in taking sides. As for me, I think that's carrying impartiality a bit far, but a judge is a judge."

"Well, I do have one opinion," said their mother.

"What's that?" asked their father. "You think it would be *nicer* if the Yankees got more hits than the Red Sox?"

"No," said their mother. "It has nothing to do with baseball. It has to do with Saundra. Saundra doesn't look well."

"We've been through this before," said Saundra.

"Your mother's right, princess," said their father. "You don't look well. You look—you look a little worse. Is something the matter?"

"I don't know," said Saundra.

"She's—" Lily began.

"Don't say anything, Lily," Saundra said and gave her almost the kind of glare she used to give her before they had become friends.

"Okay," said Lily. "I won't."

"What's going on here?" asked their father. "What do you know that we don't?"

"Nothing," said Saundra.

"Nothing," said Lily.

"I don't believe you—either of you," said their mother. "What is this little secret between the two of you?"

"Maybe we shouldn't ask, Judge," said their father. "It's the first time I can remember them sharing anything."

"That's true," said their mother. "But if they want to share something, let it be something other than a secret. There should be no secrets in our family. No whispering, no private agreements, no keeping things from the rest of us; in short, no sec—"

"I'm scared," Saundra interrupted.

"What?" asked their mother and their father at the same time.

Saundra shook her head. She didn't want to say anything more.

"She said . . ." Lily began. Then she stopped and bent down so that she could look into Saundra's face. "Is it all right if I say it?" she asked her sister.

Saundra nodded.

But before Lily could say anything more, her mother said, "I heard her. It's not that I didn't hear her. It's just that I don't understand. Do you understand?" she asked her husband.

"I guess not," he said.

"Do you?" Lily's mother asked her.

Lily nodded.

"Then what is it?" asked her mother.

Lily was about to say something when Saundra raised her head and said, "Never mind, Lily." Then she said to her parents, "I don't know what's the matter with me. I'm scared all the time. I'm nervous. I'm losing too much weight. I don't have any energy. I feel weak and tired."

"Don't think we haven't noticed," said their father. "We've been worried about you."

"At least it's out in the open now," their mother said. "Available for discussion."

Saundra said nothing. There was no expression on her face. Their parents looked at her, their faces begging her to speak. But still Saundra said nothing.

"It's the audition," said their father. "You're training too hard, wearing yourself out."

"You must slow down," said their mother. "By this time next week it will be all over. And you'll be in the company or you won't be in the company."

"We'll love you regardless," said their father.

"We certainly shall," their mother agreed.

"You will?" asked Saundra. Everyone, including Lily, was startled to hear her speak.

"Of course," said their father and mother together.

"It doesn't matter whether I get into the company or I don't get into the company?" asked Saundra.

"Not to us," said their father. "We love you anyway, princess. Does it matter to you?"

"I don't know," replied Saundra.

"I think it matters," said their father. "I think you're just *saying* you don't know if it matters because you're frightened."

"Of what?" asked their mother.

"Of losing," said their father to their mother. "Of losing," said their father to Saundra. "Am I right?"

Saundra said nothing.

"Am I right?" their father asked again.

Without looking up, Saundra said, in a tiny voice, "Ask Lily."

"What about it, Lily?" asked their father. "Is Saundra frightened of losing? Is that why she's been so upset lately?"

"She's frightened," said Lily. "But not just of losing."

"What else is she frightened of?" asked their mother.

"Of winning," said Lily.

"I don't think you're right," their father said to Lily.

"She's right," said Saundra. She turned and started to leave the room.

"Kisses," said their father.

"And hugs," said their mother.

Both girls kissed their parents, who seemed to give Saundra extra-hard hugs. Lily wasn't jealous. She was glad. Saundra needed all the help she could get.

"To hell with baseball," they heard their mother say as they walked toward their bedroom. The sound of all the screaming fans died in their ears as the TV set was turned off and their mother began to talk to their father in a quiet, worried voice.

·16·
The Sisters Impossible

They sat on Lily's bed this time.

"How did you know I'm afraid of winning too?" asked Saundra.

"I don't know. I just guessed."

"It's funny, isn't it? Being afraid of losing and winning at the same time."

"I guess," said Lily.

"I always knew I was afraid of losing. Of course I never told anybody. But I was always afraid of losing."

"Nobody likes to lose," said Lily.

"That's not true," said Saundra.

"You mean some people *like* to lose?" asked Lily.

"I don't know if they *like* to. But they're only happy

when they do. They kind of *have* to lose. They make themselves lose."

"Does that mean they're afraid of winning?" asked Lily.

"I guess," said Saundra.

"Well, you're afraid of winning," said Lily. "Does that mean you have to lose? Does that mean you're going to make yourself lose?"

"No."

"How come?"

"Because I'm not like them. I won't be *happy* if I lose."

"Will you be happy if you win?"

"I don't know. I guess I'll be happier if I win than if I lose."

"Then why are you afraid of winning?" asked Lily.

"I don't know," said Saundra.

"I do," said Lily.

"*You* do?"

For a moment, Saundra sounded just like her old haughty self. Lily wanted to stick her tongue out at her, but she realized her sister couldn't help sounding haughty sometimes and that she wasn't really haughty. She had never been really haughty. She had only learned to seem haughty, so people wouldn't know she was scared.

"That's right," Lily said. "I do. Little old me."

"Why, then?" Saundra asked.

"I don't think I'll tell you," said Lily.

"Don't tease me," said Saundra. "Please don't tease me."

"I'm sorry," said Lily. "I don't mean to tease you. I didn't even know I *could* tease you. I didn't know you were teasable."

"Now you know," said Saundra.

"Gee," said Lily.

"Big deal," said Saundra. "So I'm teasable. There are a lot of things I am that you don't know about."

"Like what?" asked Lily.

"You'll have to find out for yourself," said Saundra. "You're doing a pretty good job already."

"What do you mean?"

"You know I'm teasable. You know I'm afraid of losing. You know I'm afraid of winning. You know I'm scared of Meredith Meredith. You know I'm always putting on an act."

"You are?"

"Most of the time."

"Gee," said Lily.

"But not now."

"I know," said Lily.

"See. You even know that."

Lily smiled. She hadn't really thought about whether Saundra might be putting on an act, but she knew she wasn't.

"I like you better this way," said Lily.

"You do, huh? You like me better when I'm skinny

and tired and nervous and scared? Some friend you are."

"I like you better when you're not putting on an act," Lily said.

"Me too," said Saundra. "But tell me something else, Lily."

"What?"

"Why am I afraid of winning?"

"Well . . ." Lily began. She stopped. She didn't want to say it.

"Go ahead," Saundra ordered.

"I think you're afraid of growing up," Lily said. "That's why you're afraid of winning. If you win a place in the company, you'll be almost like a grown-up."

"Gee," said Saundra. "You're right."

"As usual," Lily said. But what a thing to say. What a haughty thing to say. And how curiously good it felt to say it. She said it again. "As usual."

"You're impossible!" said Saundra.

"I know," said Lily.

"How about me?" asked Saundra.

"You're impossible too," said Lily. "You were always impossible."

"I know," said Saundra.

"We're both impossible," said Lily.

Saundra laughed. Then she asked: "Do you want me to win or do you want me to lose?"

"I want you to win."

"Will you be jealous if I win?"

"No."

"What will you be?"

"Proud."

"And if I win, and I become a grown-up, an adult, will you like that too?"

"Maybe," said Lily.

"Why just 'maybe'? "

"I won't like it if you don't show me how to be grown up myself. I will like it if you do."

"I will," said Saundra.

"Really?" asked Lily. "You won't treat me like a kid?"

"You are a kid."

Lily patted her body and then got up from the bed and pretended to measure herself. "You're right," she said. "I am a kid. Still—"

"Don't worry," Saundra interrupted. "I won't treat you like one."

"What will you treat me like?"

"Like what you are. My dear little sister who's going to help me win."

"How?"

"By beating up Meredith Meredith."

Lily knew that Saundra wasn't serious about her beating up Meredith Meredith. And yet . . .

Well, Saundra didn't want her to *hit* Meredith

Meredith. For one thing, the one time Lily had hit her, it had been almost an accident—Lily hadn't thought about hitting her, she had just done it. And for another thing, Saundra knew as well as Lily that Meredith Meredith was strong enough and big enough to beat up Lily in a real fight. The only reason Meredith Meredith hadn't done so last time was because she had been so surprised when Lily slapped her that she just stood there, frozen like a statue.

Saundra didn't want Lily to get beat up. So she didn't want Lily to hit Meredith Meredith. What she wanted Lily to do, she said, was to "intimidate" Meredith Meredith.

"What does that mean?" Lily asked the next day when Saundra used the word on the bus on the way to school.

"To scare her," Saundra replied.

"How am *I* going to scare her?"

"You have to threaten her. Make her afraid."

"Of *me?* " Lily asked.

"Hmmm," said Saundra, looking at little Lily. "I suppose not. Anyway, it's not *you* she should be scared of. It's me."

"Then *you* intimidate her," said Lily, hoping Saundra would immediately agree.

"Not me," she said.

"Why not? You just said it's you she should be scared of."

"I know. But I want her to be scared of me during

the audition. I want her to be scared of me as a dancer."

"Maybe she is already. You're a better dancer than she is."

"No I'm not," said Saundra.

Lily couldn't believe her ears. "You're not?"

"No. She's better than I am. Not a lot better. But better."

"But I thought—"

"I know," Saundra interrupted. "I've always tried to pretend that I'm better. But I always knew, deep down inside, that she's better."

"No wonder you're scared of her."

"I know," said Saundra.

"No wonder you've been such a mess."

"Who's a mess?" said Saundra. She made her voice sound angry, but Lily knew from the way Saundra was looking at her that she knew Lily was right.

"All summer," said Lily. "The closer it's gotten to the audition—"

"—the more of a mess I've become," Saundra said. "You're right."

"Yup," said Lily.

"And now I have a week to pull myself together."

Lily just nodded. She wondered how Saundra was going to be able to do it. She wondered what she herself could possibly do to help.

"Here's our stop," said Saundra, rising from her seat. She held out her hand, and Lily took it. It was a wonderful feeling. It was so good to be friends with her sister.

"You can win," said Lily, as they started to walk down 66th Street.

Saundra said nothing. But it wasn't like her silence of the past. It didn't exclude Lily. It surrounded her in the sad quiet of Saundra's mind.

"You can win," Lily said again. "But you have to stand up straight."

Saundra looked at her, took a deep breath, threw her shoulders back, straightened her spine, stuck her chin up, and began to walk with the long strides that used to make Lily feel left behind.

"I guess you have to be haughty," Lily whispered, more to herself than to Saundra.

"What?"

"Nothing," said Lily, thinking that maybe it was also true you must look like a dancer to be a dancer.

She had to walk with quick steps to keep up with Saundra, but this time she found it fun to do. It was good to see Saundra coming alive again. Lily didn't mind having to work hard to avoid being left behind.

What she did mind was not knowing how to help Saundra. Intimidate Meredith Meredith? How was she ever going to do that?

·17·
Intimidation

She did it by talking to Meredith Meredith.

But first she talked to her father.

"Dad, I have a problem," she said.

He was lying on his bedroom floor doing sit-ups. He always did sit-ups now before he went jogging around the reservoir. He said it was the best way to attack his "problem area." No one in the family had to ask what that meant: first, he still had a very round stomach; second, whenever he said "problem area," he rubbed his very round stomach.

He wore his red jogging suit and green sneakers when he did his sit-ups. He hooked the sneakers under the bed frame to try to keep his legs flat against the floor. He was beginning to succeed. When he'd first started to do sit-ups, his legs would bend at the knees, and the bed would actually move toward him. Lily used to sit on the bed so it wouldn't move. Now she was sitting on it again, but this time so she could talk to him. He didn't need her any longer to keep the bed in place. His stomach was actually getting stronger, and flatter.

"A problem?" he said, lifting himself toward where she sat. "What kind of problem?"

"Well, I can't mention any names," she said.

"Not even to me?" As he said this, his head curved away from Lily and back down toward the floor. It was like talking to someone who's on a swing.

"Not even to you," she said.

Now he just lay on the floor, taking deep breaths. "Keeping secrets from me? Your old dad?"

"Not secrets," Lily said. "I just can't mention any names. It's not secret. It's just private."

He smiled. "A valid distinction," he said. Lily was about to ask what that meant when he added: "You certainly are a smart kid."

She decided she'd ask him another time. He might as well think she was smarter than she knew she really was. So she just smiled back.

"So what's your problem?" he asked. "And remember: no names."

"Thanks, Dad," she said. Then she asked him, "Do you know what 'intimidate' means?"

"Sure," he said. "Do you?"

"Sure," she said. "But suppose you had to intimidate someone who was bigger than you and stronger than you and also was a mean and nasty person with a dirty mouth who didn't like you in the first place and already had a reason for wanting to beat you up. What would you do?"

"I think I'd run away," said her father.

"Seriously, Dad." She didn't want him to joke at a time like this. "What would you do? How would you intimidate this person?"

"Not with my fists," he said.

"You're right about that," Lily said, relieved.

"So what does that leave you?" he said. Then he answered his own question: "Your mouth. And I don't mean biting. I mean talking."

Lily nodded. So far they agreed.

"You can always do more with talking than with fighting anyway. Words," he said. "There's an old expression: 'The pen is mightier than the sword.' Well, the tongue is mightier than the fist. Not that you'd want to stand there in the gym banging your tongue against a punching bag." He chuckled.

"Seriously, Dad," Lily said again, to get him back on the subject.

"Okay," he said. "Here's what we've established so far: You'll have to intimidate whoever it is by talking. You'll have to use your mouth. Which means you'll have to use your head. Your mouth is only as good as your brain."

"But how can you really intimidate someone by talking to them?" Lily asked.

"You can tell them they're terrible, awful, no good, rotten, a total failure, and a loser from beginning to end." His voice grew louder as he said all this, and when he was finished he did a fast sit-up. Then he lay still again, out of breath from talking and his zippy sit-up.

"But supposing the person isn't," Lily said. "Supposing the person is actually very good at the thing you're trying to intimidate them about."

"Then you really do have a problem," he said.

"I told you I did," said Lily.

"That's true," he said. "But maybe we can still solve it."

"How?"

"Well, you have to give up the idea of intimidating this person."

"But I *can't,* " said Lily. And she couldn't. Saundra was counting on her.

"You have to," said her father. "But listen to me. You may not be able to intimidate this person. But maybe you can make this person intimidate herself."

He'd guessed it was a girl. He was very smart. But Lily decided not to try to make him believe he was wrong. So once again she simply asked, "How?"

"Well, if this person thinks she's so good, then you have to make her believe that she's even better than she is. You have to make her see herself almost as if she were not herself but were perfect. And both you and I know, Lily, that no one's perfect. But if someone believes she's perfect, then she's not only not perfect, but she's an automatic failure. She'll be overconfident, and overconfidence always leads to failure. I've seen it all my life."

"You mean I should intimidate her by telling her she's terrific?"

"You not only have to tell her. You have to make her believe it. And I mean really believe it. Of course, she won't *really* believe in herself. She'll just believe in your *telling* her to believe in herself. Deep inside she'll be both overconfident and underconfident at the same time."

"But how can I do all that?" Lily asked.

"As you said when you came in here, you've got a problem." Her father began to do his sit-ups again.

"How can I solve it?"

"I think you already know *how*. Now you just need to do it. Use your head. Use that mouth of yours. You can do it." As he said this, he closed his eyes, pressed his lips together, and rose from and fell to the floor like a man who had his own problem to solve.

She had to use her mouth. She'd known it all along. Well, she wasn't going to bite Meredith Meredith, and she wasn't going to bang her tongue against her, so all that was left was to talk to her.

It was a real chance to take.

First of all, she had no idea how Meredith Meredith would react. Talk to the little girl who had slapped her! Lily could imagine that Meredith Meredith might slap her right back.

Second, she didn't know how Saundra would react. She was afraid that Saundra would see her with Meredith Meredith and would misunderstand and get angry with her all over again. And if Saundra didn't get angry at just seeing Lily talking to Meredith Meredith, surely she would blow her top if she heard what Lily was going to say to Meredith Meredith.

Lily couldn't take the chance. Not the whole chance. She was too afraid of having her sister turn against her. So, without telling her the plan for intimidating Meredith Meredith, she said to her sister: "No matter what you hear about what I say to Meredith Meredith, don't believe it."

"What do you mean?" asked Saundra, speaking through the shoulder loop of her white leotard, which she was putting on for the rehearsal for her audition. "Don't believe you've said it, whatever it is you're going to say?"

"No," said Lily. "Don't believe I *mean* it."

"I can hardly believe you're going to talk to her, Lily! What are you going to say?"

"None of your business."

"It is too," Saundra replied, gliding a slipper onto her foot with one finger.

"Well," said Lily, "maybe it is your business. But

why don't you just let Meredith Meredith be my business for a while, and you take care of your *other* business."

"What other business?"

"Dancing," said Lily.

Saundra didn't answer her, not with words. But as she put on her other slipper and pulled her hair back perfectly with one sweep of her hand—oh, how Lily was jealous of the way she did that—she nodded her head and seemed to be thinking. She didn't say a word. She just kept nodding and kept looking into herself as she rose from the bench and went off to rehearsal.

As soon as Saundra was gone, Lily found Meredith Meredith's dance bag, which had her initials on it just like Saundra's (MMM—Lily wondered what Meredith Meredith's middle name might be, and giggled), and she left a note in the bag.

It said: *If you want to find out how to win the audition, talk to Lily Leonard in private after class.*

And, just to be safe, she added a postscript: *P.S. Lily Leonard is sorry she slapped your face.*

Then Lily went to her own class, where she learned an arabesque *fondue*, which Miss Witt explained was the same as an arabesque *plié*, one leg held up and behind her, the other on the floor and bending at the knee.

Several people in class fell down while trying to sink toward the floor, including Yuri, of course. But this time he didn't laugh. He seemed to have changed nearly overnight. Lily had been watching him since the beginning. He had learned to do a few things almost well. And now, though he had made another embarrassing mistake, he didn't hide his head, he didn't laugh at himself. He frowned, he scowled, and he picked himself up very quickly and tried the arabesque *fondue* again. Again he stumbled, but this time he kept himself from falling to the floor. Again he tried it. Again he stumbled. He shook his head, scowled, and talked to himself. Lily wasn't sure, but she thought she heard him whisper, "Jerk." And then he tried it again. Lily wanted to walk over to him and tell him that maybe for the first time since school had begun, he *wasn't* a jerk—for the first time he was behaving like a real dancer. But she couldn't leave her place and couldn't stop trying herself.

She found it very difficult to do an arabesque *fondue* and hated the feeling of being awkward. Mrs. Howell came over to help her, but it didn't do much good. Lily could bend her right leg enough to get to about a demi-*plié* position, but her left leg was too weak to allow her to move down and still keep her balance. Her knee hurt. She realized, once again, how hard it was to dance and how much of a beginner she was.

This was Hector's last class with Miss Witt's beginners. The little boy in the green leotard was being moved to an advanced group. Lily watched him during class and tried to dance the way he did. But it was hopeless. There was no better way to find out how good you were than to compare yourself, right there on the floor, in class, with another dancer. She was jealous of Hector, for she would have loved to be moved to an advanced group. But the more she watched him, the more she understood why he was leaving and she was staying with the beginners. He was better than anyone else in the class.

If she really was going to be a dancer, she would have to become not only better than she was now but better than almost all the other people in the class, the way Hector was better. But Hector was better not only because he seemed to practice a lot. Hector was better also because . . . he was just better. "A born dancer," Miss Witt once said to Mrs. Howell about him. Lily knew that she herself was not a born dancer. It didn't seem fair. But what Hector was born with, Lily would have to find in her body and her mind now, when she had been alive nearly ten whole years. Hector had so much of a head start on her. How could she ever catch up? And what if he just kept getting better and better? She would never catch up.

It was so discouraging. She really liked Hector, but she didn't want him to be so much better than she was. She wanted him to be worse. She wanted to be the best.

She felt afraid all of a sudden as she watched Hector. She knew he was better than she was, and she felt afraid. And he was a boy! Suppose he was a girl.

Then Lily and this girl-Hector would be trying out for the same roles, maybe for the same place in the company someday. And Lily knew that she would lose. It was very scary.

No wonder Saundra was scared of Meredith Meredith. There was only one place in the second company, and there were five girls trying out for it. Saundra admitted that Meredith Meredith was a better dancer than she was. No wonder she was scared. Dancing seemed so pure. If someone was better than you, then they were better. There was nothing you could do about it, except practice some more and hope that you got better while the other person didn't.

Well, there wasn't time for Saundra to practice very much before the audition. If Meredith Meredith was a better dancer, then Meredith Meredith was going to get the place in the company, and Saundra wouldn't. What was Lily going to do?

As she walked toward the dressing room after class, feeling discouraged about Hector and her own dancing and Saundra's chances of beating out Meredith Meredith, she felt a hand on her arm. She knew without looking who it was.

"I should break your nose," said Meredith Meredith, who was dressed in her leotard and tights and was chewing gum and was sweating, as Lily herself was sweating.

Lily felt like putting her hands over her face, just in case.

"But then you'd be even more funny-looking," Meredith Meredith went on. "You could get a job in a freak show and get rich. And I don't want you to be rich. So I'm not going to break your nose."

"Gee, thanks," Lily said without thinking, because she was so relieved. She didn't realize right away how funny it sounded. What she did realize was that she was over her first worry: that Meredith Meredith would hit her to get even for Lily's slapping her in the face.

Meredith Meredith laughed scornfully. "What am I supposed to say? You're welcome? Boy, you are a dumb kid."

"I know it," said Lily, trying to be agreeable.

"What?" Meredith Meredith looked as if she couldn't believe her ears.

"I know I'm a dumb kid."

Meredith Meredith shook her head. "Anyone who calls themselves dumb must really be dumb."

"But if you're dumb, and you know you're dumb," Lily said, "then you must be smart."

"Why?"

"Because you know."

Meredith Meredith looked confused. She chewed even harder on her gum. Her large lips seemed to be crawling back and forth across the bottom of her face like fat pink worms.

"Yeah, but you don't go around admitting it," she said.

"That means you're honest," said Lily.

"So what does that make *you?* " asked Meredith Meredith.

"Smart—"

"Smart?"

"—and honest," Lily concluded.

"So now you're smart and honest?" said Meredith Meredith.

"Yup."

"And not dumb?"

"Nope."

"Well, if you're so smart," said Meredith Meredith, putting her face near Lily's, near enough so Lily could smell the peppermint from Meredith Meredith's gum and the sweat from her skin, "then tell me how I'm going to win the audition."

"Do you think you're going to win it?"

"Of course I do."

"Then you don't need me to tell you how to do it," Lily said.

"What about this note?" Meredith Meredith said, pulling it out from the top of her leotard.

"It was a mistake," Lily said.

"What do you mean, a mistake?"

"I thought you wanted to know how to win."

"I *do*, " said Meredith Meredith, so loudly that when she heard herself, she looked around, as if embarrassed to be almost screaming.

"But you already think you're going to win."

"Of course I do."

"Then you don't need me to tell you how to do it," Lily repeated.

"Yes I do!" Meredith Meredith said, not seeming to care now who might hear her.

"Why?"

"I just do. Don't ask me why. I just do. So tell me."

"First tell me why," said Lily.

"No."

"Okay. Then I won't tell you how."

"You better!" said Meredith Meredith. And she put one of her hands on Lily's hip. It wasn't squeezing. At least not yet.

And the other hand . . . Now Lily knew why Meredith Meredith hadn't put both her hands on Lily's hips. Meredith Meredith's other hand was hovering up near her own face. Meredith Meredith was afraid that Lily would slap her again. Meredith Meredith was afraid. Of me! Lily thought. She was intimidated! What a shame that Lily had to do more than intimidate her. She also had to make her overconfident, make her believe in herself without really believing in herself.

"Let go," said Lily, "and I'll tell you how to win."

"You will?"

"Sure."

"Why are you going to tell me how to beat out your own sister?"

Lily was prepared for that question. She just wasn't

sure that her answer would work. "Because she's haughty," she said.

"What does that mean?" asked Meredith Meredith.

"Stuck-up," Lily explained, and it took all her restraint to keep from telling Meredith Meredith that she might be beautiful, and she might be a terrific dancer, but she certainly was dumb.

"She sure is!" said Meredith Meredith, smiling so that her lips crawled almost halfway up the sides of her nose.

And Lily knew that her answer had worked. "Haughty," she repeated, like a teacher trying to help a little kid learn a new word.

"Wow, I'm glad to hear you say it," said Meredith Meredith, finally taking her hand from Lily's hip. "Everybody in the school thinks so. Even her own sister. . . . She is *so* stuck-up."

"But she doesn't deserve to be," Lily said.

"She doesn't?" Meredith Meredith asked. "How come?"

"Because she's not the best dancer." Lily let out her breath. That was the hardest thing of all to say.

"She's not?" Meredith Meredith seemed surprised.

"Nope," said Lily.

"Who is?" asked Meredith Meredith, leaning down toward Lily, as if a secret were about to be told. Her mouth was hanging open, like that of a dog about to be fed.

"You," said Lily, and nearly choked on the little word.

"Me?" Meredith Meredith looked as if she didn't believe it. Then she caught herself looking that way, straightened up, and said, "Me. Of course."

"Of course," echoed Lily.

"But . . ." Meredith Meredith began. "But how do you know?"

"*Everyone* knows."

"They do?"

"Sure," said Lily.

"Who's everyone?"

Gee, what a dope, thought Lily. Aloud, she said, "Everyone is everyone."

"What about Saundra? Does she think I'm the best?"

"Yup," said Lily.

"She does?"

"Yup."

Meredith Meredith stood up straight again and took a step away from Lily and looked into her face as if she suddenly didn't believe a word she'd said. "How do you know?" she asked.

"She told me."

"She told you she thinks I'm a better dancer than she is?"

"Yes," said Lily, and despite the fact that it was the absolute truth, Lily found the word as difficult to say as if it had been a lie. "And you know what?" she said, gulping, about to say something that was even more difficult.

"What?" Meredith Meredith's eyes were as wide as melon balls.

"You *are* better." Lily nearly choked on the words.

"You think so?" asked Meredith Meredith, suddenly drawing her body up so that she looked ten feet tall and squinting down at Lily from both sides of her nose as if Lily were an ant on the floor and very hard to find.

"You're a terrific dancer," Lily said.

"Why thank you," said Meredith Meredith. She paused. Then she asked, "*How* terrific?"

"The best," Lily said. She wanted to cross her fingers behind her back, but she was afraid Meredith Meredith would see her and ruin her whole intimidation plan.

"And better than Saundra, right?"

"Right," said Lily.

"I *knew* it!" Meredith Meredith almost screamed.

"Of course you knew it," said Lily. "You're smart." *Yikes!* What a lie, she thought. It was all she could do to keep from crossing her eyes and giving Meredith Meredith a look that would make her punch Lily in the nose.

"I know it," said Meredith Meredith. "I'm smart. I'm very smart."

"And a very good dancer," Lily reminded her, in case she had forgotten the important thing.

"The best," said Meredith Meredith. "Everyone knows that."

"Everyone," Lily said.

"Absolutely everyone," said Meredith Meredith. "Even your sister."

"Even her," said Lily. "*Especially* her."

"Right," said Meredith Meredith.

"And she's your only competition for the place in the company," Lily said.

"She *was* my only competition," Meredith Meredith corrected her.

"She *was* your only competition," Lily mimicked her.

"But not anymore," said Meredith Meredith.

"Not anymore," said Lily.

Now she had Meredith Meredith just where she wanted her. Now Meredith Meredith herself was convinced that she was best.

"You don't have to practice anymore," said Lily.

"Of course I don't. I don't have any competition."

"No competition," said Lily.

"I'm the best."

"The best," said Lily.

"There's no *way* I can lose."

"No way," said Lily.

"I don't even have to try. I can beat her with my eyes closed."

"With your eyes closed," said Lily.

"I'm the winner!" Meredith Meredith shrieked.

"The winner," said Lily softly.

"Bye," said Meredith Meredith, and she turned on her heels without giving Lily another glance.

"Bye," said Lily. And only when she was sure that Meredith Meredith was completely out of sight did she stick out her tongue at her and cross her fingers behind her back and cross her eyes and let her lips droop and take a deep breath of triumph.

·18·
A Born Something

When Lily found Saundra in the dressing room, Saundra didn't look at all happy.

Lily couldn't wait to give her the good news and cheer her up. But before Lily could say a word, Saundra said angrily, "What did you say to Meredith Meredith?"

Uh oh, thought Lily and realized that her warning to Saundra had done no good: Saundra had heard what she'd said to Meredith Meredith, and she *did* believe it.

"None of your business," said Lily.

"Don't try that again on me, Lily. It *is* my business. And I want to know what you said to her."

"I'm not *telling*," Lily said in as strong a voice as she could muster in her disappointment.

"Well, *don't*, then," said Saundra. "You don't have to. Because I already know."

"Good for you," said Lily.

"And do you want to know *how* I know?" asked Saundra, ignoring Lily's snotty remark. "I know because everybody is talking about it. Meredith Meredith is telling everybody. Look."

Saundra pointed across the room, where Meredith Meredith was surrounded by a group of girls who were listening intently to her while Meredith Meredith moved her big lips up and down and at the same time pointed over to Saundra and Lily. Then she left that group of girls and rushed over to another. Again she pointed to Saundra and Lily. Again her lips showed that she was talking a mile a minute.

"Good," said Lily. "I'm glad she's telling everyone."

"But you don't even know what she's saying."

"Yes I do," said Lily.

"You do?"

"She's telling them that she's going to beat you out for the place in the company."

"Big deal," replied Saundra. "She's *always* said that."

"She's telling them that she's a better dancer than you."

"She's always said that too."

Lily took a deep breath. "She's telling them that *I* said she's going to beat you out. She's telling them that

I said she's a better dancer than you. She's telling them that *I* said she can beat you with—"

"With her eyes closed!" Saundra snapped. "Then it's *true* that you—"

"Wow," Lily interrupted. "Meredith Meredith didn't forget a word. That's terrific."

Saundra opened her mouth to speak, but Lily didn't give her a chance. "And it *is* true that I told her all those things. But I didn't think it would work so well. Look at her, Saundra"—Lily pointed right back at Meredith Meredith—"look at her. She's so proud of herself. She really *does* think she's going to win."

Suddenly Saundra wasn't angry any longer. She was sad. As she spoke, her voice almost cracked with tears. "I know it," she said. "She thinks she's going to win. And I don't think I'm going to win. I don't."

"But she's not going to win," Lily said.

"But you *told* her she's going to win. My own sister."

"I know I did. And she believed me. It wasn't easy, but I made her believe me. At first she didn't believe she was going to win. That's why she was willing to talk to me in the first place. I left her a note saying that I would tell her how to win. But I didn't. I didn't tell her *how* to win. I just told her she *would* win. And she believed me. She really did." Lily smiled. "She doesn't believe in herself, Saundra. But she was stupid enough to believe what I told her. Look at how confident she seems. Look at what she's drinking."

And it was true. Meredith Meredith was standing in the midst of yet another group of girls, and she was drinking a Coke.

"A Coke!" said Saundra.

"Can you believe it!" said Lily.

"Sugar!" said Saundra, starting to laugh.

"Ugh!" said Lily.

"But wait a minute," said Saundra, no longer laughing. "You told her you'd tell her how to win?"

"Yes."

"And she believed you?"

"I guess so."

Now Saundra really started to laugh.

"What's so funny about that?" Lily asked. Her feelings were hurt.

"Oh, Lily," Saundra said and put her hands on Lily's shoulders. "I'm sorry I'm laughing. Really I am. It's just funny. I'm sorry, but it's funny. Meredith Meredith has been dancing for almost ten years. You've been dancing for a few weeks. You couldn't tell her how to win if she didn't know already."

"That's true," said Lily.

"What? You admit it? I didn't hurt your feelings?"

"You always hurt someone's feelings when you laugh at them," Lily said. "But you're right. I couldn't tell her how to win if she didn't know already. And she didn't know. And she still doesn't."

"I hope you're right."

"I am. But even more important, I can tell *you* how to win."

"Lily . . ." Saundra wasn't laughing now.

"I can," said Lily. "And I learned it from Meredith Meredith."

"What did you learn from Meredith Meredith?"

"I learned she didn't think she was going to win. I learned she was scared of you. And so I learned that she was just like you. *You* don't think you're going to win. And *you're* scared of *her*. The only difference is, now she's absolutely confident she's going to win, and she's not scared of you any longer. But she doesn't believe it deep down inside herself. She only believes it because I told her. And that's how I intimidated her."

"It doesn't sound very intimidating to me," said Saundra.

"You're right," said Lily. Now Saundra was beginning to understand. "It wasn't really intimidation. She's too big. I *couldn't* intimidate her. Anyway, I didn't really want to intimidate her. I wanted her to intimidate herself. And now she's going to."

"She's going to intimidate herself?" asked Saundra. "How?"

"By forgetting who she is. By thinking she's better than she is. By seeing in her mind another Meredith Meredith who's such a good dancer that the real Meredith Meredith believes she doesn't have to practice anymore and she can't lose. It's okay to think you can win. But it's not okay to think you can't lose. You intimidate yourself when you think you can't lose. You may not scare yourself, but you threaten yourself, and that's intimidation. You said so yourself."

"Wait a minute," said Saundra. She looked puzzled.

"What's the matter? Don't you understand?" Lily asked.

"I'm not sure," said Saundra.

"If you're not sure, then you don't understand."

"Boy, are you tough," said Saundra. "Okay, so I don't understand. I never said I was as smart as you are. Everybody knows you're the smart kid in the family. But it's one thing to be smart. It's another thing to be tough. What happened to my little sister? How did you get so tough?"

Lily listened to Saundra and realized that she was not kidding. Saundra was really calling her smart and tough. Saundra was really saying that she thought Lily was smarter than she was. Lily had never realized before that Saundra thought that way, and she had certainly never realized that Saundra might feel bad about it, about not being as smart as her little sister. And Lily suddenly knew that it was true. She *was* smarter than Saundra. She knew more than Saundra. Her brain worked faster than Saundra's brain. Part of the reason was that Saundra had been dancing every day for six years. But another part was that Lily was just smarter, the way little Hector was just better as a dancer. Lily was born smarter the way Hector was born a dancer. She had a mind that could dance.

But her body . . . It was true that she now felt strong and thin and limber. But she was not a dancer. She was not a born dancer. She knew that when autumn came, she would no longer go to dancing class every day. Maybe on Saturdays, but not every day. Saundra was the dancer in the family. Saundra's life was the dance, and it would be even more so when she won the audition. But Lily didn't want her life to be the dance. It didn't feel right to her to take up so much time and energy trying to become something that she might never be. She didn't want to have to win auditions against people like Meredith Meredith. She didn't want to worry, every time she ate an ice cream cone, that she was committing a sin against her body. Even more, she didn't want to be disappointed in the end.

For, deep down inside, Lily knew that she was not good enough to be a truly great dancer. She was not like Hector and, maybe, Saundra. Lily was a born something, she knew, but she didn't know quite yet what that something was. Maybe a lawyer, like her father. Maybe a lawyer *and* a judge, like her mother. Something. She would have to wait to find out. In the meantime, she would try a lot of things. As many things as possible. In this she would be different from Saundra, who only danced. But that was all right. Some people find one thing very early and devote their whole lives to it. Other people experiment with many things and hope to find something someday that they love and are good at. If they don't, they'll at least have lived a full life and learned a great deal. That was fine with Lily. There was so much she wanted to do. There was more, even, than she could imagine right now. How wonderful it was to think she would be doing things she'd never even heard of. How wonderful to think of her life ahead.

She could be anything. But tough? Lily didn't feel tough. Except—she did feel tougher than she used to. After all, it was she who used to be scared of Saundra the way Saundra was scared of Meredith Meredith. But now she was no longer scared. So maybe she was tough.

To Saundra she said, "I got tough from dancing."

Saundra nodded. "I believe that's true."

"But if I were in the audition, I wouldn't be so tough. I'd be scared too."

"You would?"

"I'd be scared of losing. You're scared of losing, aren't you, Saundra?"

"I guess."

"Everyone is," Lily said. "Unless they're stupid. Meredith Meredith is stupid. Look at her. She's not scared anymore, she thinks she can't lose. That's because I'm smarter than she is. And that's why you're going to win."

"I am?"

"Yup."

"How?"

"Practice," Lily said.

"Practice? But I already—"

"Not that kind of practice," Lily said. "You already do enough of that kind of practice. Maybe too much. Remember about peaking."

"So what kind of practice are you talking about?"

"In your mind," Lily said. "You have to believe in yourself, really believe. Not like Meredith Meredith. *You* have to believe in *you.*"

"I wish I could."

"You can do it," Lily said, just as her father had said to her.

"How?"

"Come with me," Lily said and held out her hand.

Saundra took it, and the two of them moved through the crowd of noisy, gum-chewing, sweaty girls, moved out through the door of the dressing room, walked through the corridors until they found an empty practice room.

And there, while Lily sat on the teacher's stool, Saundra danced for her, performing the routine she would do for her audition. And while she danced, Lily told her over and over again that she would win, that she would win because she was the best, that she would win because she deserved to win, that she would win because she believed she would win.

As Saundra danced, Lily herself came to believe

that she would win. She had had no idea how good Saundra was. She could hardly believe her eyes.

The more Saundra danced, the better she became. Her body seemed to get stronger and to open up. The muscles in her legs and back and shoulders pushed out through the skin and glistened with sweat. The summer light coming in through the large window at the far end of the room curved around Saundra's body and reflected off its wetness and seemed to become her partner in the dance.

Lily could hear Saundra humming the music to which she would dance her audition. She was breathing hard, and her voice cracked and was higher than usual but it still sounded beautiful. She was singing a song that only she and Lily could hear, a private melody to which her body responded as if the music were part of her and part of the dance. Saundra became the dance she was doing. She was the music and the movement, and they were Saundra.

Skinny, beautiful, graceful, haughty Saundra. Lily loved her.

"You will win," she told her.

And Lily knew that when Saundra won, she, Lily, would win too. She was part of her sister's dance. She was part of her sister's body. They were not the same people. They were very different people. But they were sisters. They belonged together. They shared their lives. And as long as they continued to share their lives, everything was possible, and they could not lose.

JAMES DAVID LANDIS is the author of several books for young readers, most recently *The Band Never Dances*. Mr. Landis was born in Springfield, Massachusetts, and now lives in New York City.